noah

THE SWISS LIST

noah

a novel of the boom times

HUGO LOETSCHER

TRANSLATED BY SAMUEL P. WILLCOCKS

LONDON NEW YORK CALCUTTA

swiss arts council

prshelvetia

This publication was supported by a grant from
Pro Helvetia, Swiss Arts Council

Seagull Books, 2012

First Published as *Noah: Roman einer Konjunktur*
© Diogenes Verlag AG, Zurich, Switzerland, 1995
All rights reserved

English translation © Samuel P. Willcocks, 2012

ISBN-13   978 0 8574 2 046 6

British Library Cataloguing-in-Publication Data
A catalogue record for this book is available from the British Library.

Typeset in Bembo Standard by Seagull Books, Calcutta, India
Printed and bound by Hyam Enterprises, Calcutta, India

No, the people of Mesopotamia had never had it so good. There had been an economic miracle: Noah had built his Ark.

But as ever, when everyone's doing well, some were doing even better.

The first architect Noah consulted had squinted thoughtfully; it really wouldn't do for him, he said, with the reputation that he had and his academic duties, to build a ship with no bow, no keel, no helm. For a while he regretted having turned down the commission but, in the end, he had no reason to complain about his earnings. He built houses for those who made money building the Ark; and, since he was an interior designer as well, he had an extra set of clients. Many people had the means to live well in times like these, and wanted to live the good life, a different life from their parents' and in-laws', and were happy for the architect to pick out the right shade of blue for their bedroom since he had made a study of which colours had a calming effect.

The man who cashed in most obviously from building the Ark was no architect at all, his colleagues scoffed at first. He was a draughtsman who had started out as a bricklayer; his girlfriend, a dressmaker with a nervous laugh, had introduced him to artistic circles, and he found that he could use a ruler just as handily as a trowel; besides which, he wanted to spare his fingernails. He set up shop on his own and carried out time-consuming sketches for architects and did their tedious calculations; from one client he learnt how to raise a roof, and from another how deep a foundation should go. When Noah came to see him, he drummed his ruler on the desk and looked with surprise in his sea-blue eyes when Noah reeled off the list of those he had already tried. He told his girlfriend of Noah's visit but instead of laughing she did a few sums in her head; the commission was most welcome for a family just settling down with their two children, especially since Noah was a man with connections, so that the draughtsman could count on being offered a real building at some point.

And, indeed, he did build his real building even before the Ark was finished: the first workers' quarter. The site where Noah had chosen to build the Ark was a long way from any settlements, and the workers lost so many hours getting to and from work that they began to ask for a monthly wage. Then the draughtsman made a deal with Noah to build a workers' village next to the Ark, a village with green spaces and sunshades, not the kind of place where these people had been used to living. The living rooms and children's rooms faced south, while the parental bedrooms faced north where it was cool. To save the women a long trek to the shops, all the houses were grouped around a big co-op store where the food was unloaded from pallets and packs. While the mothers went shopping or to get their hair done, they dropped their children off to play in the landscaped gardens and splash about in the lined ponds. A workshop was equipped where the menfolk could tinker about in their time off. The recreational workshop also had a large stage on rollers which could be pushed out, and many an evening there the villagers gathered to form a choir and sing the mournful songs of Mesopotamia.

The draughtsman was given a medal for the village: half a yellow sun behind a scaffolded outline. He was picked for the commission which met to award prizes for public-tender projects. Since more prizes were given than buildings could ever be built, the exhibition halls held models of all Mesopotamia in second-best and third-best versions. Many of his colleagues now began to talk to the draughtsman in a much friendlier manner; he was often invited to speak to the Women's Institute, and his former girlfriend, now his wife, came along on these occasions. For a great many people he had become famous as a man who had started out with nothing.

The draughtsman had never expected to get rich. Hardly had he signed the contract with Noah and estimated costs than he discovered that he had no clear idea of what the Ark might look like—and nor did his client. They took a laundry tub and tried out box-shaped Arks and Arks that were rafts with railings; they weighed them down with stones of all sorts and mulled over the advantages of smooth lines or wallowing crates. When the draughtsman sat down to draw up the plans, Noah began to talk of a second storey, and soon he was talking of another on top of that. Then came the wearisome discussions about the tween decks and various proposals for the stairs; the complete redesign of the front of the ship

to make it tall enough for an elephant; then a surprising new requirement to include hammocks,
sheds, hutches and stalls; and smaller improvements,
such as putting in portholes at all quarters of the
compass. As a result, the draughtsman was busy for
far longer than planned. At first he had often warned
Noah to stick with a plan once he'd made it; but
since then he had become a husband and a father
and he had learnt that projected costs count about as
much as a birth, meaning not at all, and that only
the improvements and additions make up the sum.

The draughtsman also earned as a middleman.
First of all, a tar boiler got in touch promising fifteen
per cent. Then a trade union leader, head of the beam-
carriers, offering five per cent. The timber merchant
said that the two of them could make a deal. The
owner of a quarry invited the draughtsman to dinner,
although he insisted as firmly as he could that there
was no chance of marble-cladding the Ark. But the
quarry owner simply asked him to put in a good
word with Noah. At the meal, the draughtsman
finally got to meet the head of the building inspec-
torate and learnt another thing: In this society, it's not
what you do, it's who you do it with.

The contract for the workers' quarter and the
ongoing work on the Ark allowed the draughtsman
to fulfil a wish that his wife had had even back when

she was a dressmaker. He bought a ramshackle cabin in a remote valley; the two of them took trips to the country, week after week, until they finally knew where they wanted their hideaway where they could invite their friends. The only real expense was getting the access road built, although it wasn't cheap either to repair the tumbledown walls in a way that still showed off their rustic charm. The draughtsman furnished the interior as a comfortable little home, using local stone for the fireplace to give it that natural look. He put on a new roof though, weatherproof.

More than with anyone else, the draughtsman worked with the timber merchant. He had worked for Noah before, as a carpenter, mending fences, building stables and byres. As a carpenter, he employed workers even when times were bad. In the evenings, he would tell his wife that he'd soon have a hundred men on payroll. But his wife showed her swollen legs and turned down his amorous attentions. The carpenter promised to send her to spas, which he duly did once he had made Noah the first shipment of timbers. He hired a cook, and soon had to ask her not to speak so familiarly with him when his children were around, although, in return, she got him to agree that she could eat at the table with them. At first the carpenter made quite sure that he inspected each timber beam himself, running his hands along the wood to check that it was planed quite smooth, for he took his contract with Noah seriously, not just because they were neighbours or because his daughter was often seen with Noah's second son. But Noah hurried the building work along so much that the carpenter found he had to put an extra clause into the contract, since he offered no guarantees for wood that had not had long enough to dry.

The carpenter earned money not just with his construction work but with felling and forestry too; he insisted on being there himself to make sure that no crooked or diseased trees were felled. Once the first woods had been cleared though, Nature lovers spoke up for Mesopotamia's forested skylines and condemned the clear-felling, saying that the countryside had been ruined, that they felt sorry for the deer and the hare that had fled to other woods. The Nature lovers fell quiet only when the draughtsman and the timber merchant chivied Noah into promising to replant further in the northwest, on hills that were still untouched, high hills that gave an even finer view of the beauties of Mesopotamia.

The foresters could rest easy too, even though they had long accused Noah of reckless logging. The lawyer was able to lend his support and calm the foresters' fears well in time, and this was not just because he and the head forester belonged to the same hunters' club. Thanks to the lawyer, the rumour that the foresters had been bribed soon died down. The lawyer was able to show that the foresters had received a per diem for their attendance at the negotiations, for which they could hardly be reproached, especially as some of them were married men with children; quite the contrary, the fact that these monies had mounted up to a tidy sum simply showed that they had not given way on the first day of talks.

The lawyer had been doing very well indeed since work on the Ark had begun; he had drawn up contracts between Noah and the draughtsman as well as between Noah and the timber merchant and he was also responsible for the workers' village which won him the trust of landlords and tenants alike. He became a specialist in questions of notice and supplementary rent monies. Many in Mesopotamia had come to have a substantial income, so that quarrels were no longer settled by mud-slinging or fisticuffs but ended up in court; many indeed had achieved not just an income but also considerable wealth, and not everyone knew how best to multiply their wealth. Advice was important here. Hardly a legacy was left now without legal advice and either party in a dispute over a will could bring the case to the high court. Nowadays it wasn't just high society who got divorced, for even the simple man could afford to pay his alimony and take a second wife. When the court in Yegerom extended its premises, Noah's lawyer made a speech at the official opening of the new courts since he was also President of the Bar Association, and was applauded by the assembled attorneys; in Mesopotamia, he said, justice is in fine fettle.

But as ever, when everyone is doing well, some are doing less well.

They came from the Turkish highlands. All their worldly goods were lashed up in goatskin bundles when they arrived; when they went home for their holidays, they carried back their earnings in camel-hair blankets. No local Mesopotamian labourer could be found dragging a tree-trunk now but he was ready to call 'Ho' while the highland Turks heaved at the ropes. Some of these highland Turks lived in tenements which the locals had long abandoned, and the foreigners paid high rents, happy to have anywhere to live at all. Others lived in great tents, wanting to spend as little money as possible. They wanted to take their earnings back with them and have a home like the Mesopotamians—although without the rivers, and not so flat.

Since these immigrant labourers came from remote areas where men and women would first meet on the day after their wedding, they had a sort of sullen eagerness about them which they would unleash at the slightest glance. When a woman went past, they would purse their narrow lips and whistle, and groom their moustaches. Mothers warned their daughters that the foreigners might go at it like rabbits but were only interested in saving for their families up in the highlands—though the highlanders turned many a mother's head as well. Even in high society, where Turks were never seen, it became chic to use phrases from their language, a language of highlanders and goatherds.

When a dam burst, the rubble usually buried foreigners; if a beam fell, it almost always killed a highland Turk, and foreigners came crashing down with the scaffolding. If you saw a working man with a bandage anywhere, you could rely on it that he only spoke broken Mesopotamian. Sometimes pit props buckled and broke or mine galleries collapsed; at the mass burials afterwards, the dear departed were all foreign workers, although there might have been a local foreman lying on a bier prominently in the middle.

These highland Turks did work that no Mesopotamian would have dreamt of undertaking. The foreigners shovelled the muck off the streets and took it out of town to burn. They emptied the cesspits and were there in the hospitals to take away the soiled bandages. Above all, the restaurateurs were happy; most of them had expanded and put mosaics on their walls but had no one left to serve the guests since, in the meantime, all the Mesopotamians had become guests themselves. The highland Turks, though, were ready to dish up plates for others to eat from and take empty plates back into the kitchen; they peeled and scraped vegetables, washed dishes, cleared and cleaned after others had had their night out. They learnt the Mesopotamian language from curse words and commands.

Amid all this general prosperity, however, one man grew ever poorer.

It was the general opinion, and many whispered it, that Noah was the richest man around. He reckoned not in camels but in caravans, and counted not in sheep but in herds. But Noah, the envy of all, had miscalculated in building the Ark.

He lived in the most splendid house in Mesopotamia, although, people argued about whether the pillars at his gate were in good taste and grumbled that he never switched on the fountains in his gardens. So it was all the more remarkable that he had commissioned a project on the scale of the Ark.

Certainly, at first, he had checked every wagon of wood that came in. But the Ark site stretched and sprawled in ways that made oversight impossible. He set up checkpoints and it took him a while to find out that a wagon would show up at several different checkpoints to be paid several times over. The court was not able to establish the total amount embezzled in this first financial scandal; even if they could have, it would hardly have helped since the culprits had long ago spent or squandered the money and were serving their time.

At first Noah had believed that he would manage with a draughtsman and a few workers. But as soon as the first scaffold went up, he realized that he needed people who knew what an angle brace was and who could handle a pole; and the more the shell began to look like a ship, the more he needed people who could tell a sheer strake from a bilge board, if the Ark was to have a skin that would keep it afloat. Even before building began he would need workers to transport the wood, and to get the wood on-site he would need to build roads.

On top of which he brought in more hands to supplement the small number he had hired at first, once he realized how slowly work was going. The time came when paying minimum wage just wasn't enough. The boom had created so many jobs that even workers who had been with the Ark from the beginning were looking around for other positions. It had become quite usual for employers to poach one another's workers, offering higher wages and shorter hours. Soon enough, the notice board on-site that proclaimed 'No Openings' was taken down and replaced by another board with details of the basic wage and bonuses.

Noah still owned enough land, though, to raise credit with just a handshake, no signature required. No one sold such tracts of land as he did but then no one who sold land earned so little on the sale. He sold the land while it was still meadow, fields or pasture; and then those who owned it next sold it at the right moment as building land. But since Noah was always selling more land and, in the end, whole estates, he could keep fewer herds and had to make do with smaller harvests.

Noah didn't head into this financial ruin on his own, however, for he had family and his wife was the first to try to save him.

When Noah said that he was planning an Ark, his wife was just serving the soup. The oldest son asked whether that was the only reason he had been asked to come, right in the middle of the millet harvest. The middle son froze, his spoon halfway. The youngest son, though, threw a corner of bread into his bowl, dunked it down with the spoon and cried out, 'Another one.' By dinnertime the youngest son wasn't laughing either. Noah had placed an order for wood and when they asked him, 'How much?' he answered, 'Fourteen forests.'

Since Noah's wife had raised her husband's sons strictly, they only grumbled and cursed once he was out of the room. Noah's wife interrupted them; he was their father, she said, and he'd always been like that, they should just let him build the Ark, then see what might happen next. Besides, she was there for them as well, wasn't she? And they'd never had cause for complaint yet.

She started saving though, that very day. When she went to the butcher's or paid the baker's bill, she would always round up the amount from her housekeeping money. She told herself: You do the cooking and cleaning and you don't get a penny for it, and all because a man married you and made you into a wife and mother. Well then, from now on, you'll be your own boss, pay your own wage and keep a little bit back—you're putting something aside for a rainy day.

One night, Noah's wife woke up with a start, gasping, she reached for her husband and found herself holding an empty pillow. Noah was standing at the window, fully dressed, leaning out. The moon cast shadows on his face, quite motionless. Noah's wife sat up in bed then and wondered who he was talking to, but he stretched his hand out, as though testing for rain. She listened but couldn't hear a drop. When he left the room, she threw a shawl around herself and followed.

At first it looked as though he was just strolling in the garden but then he left through the garden gate. By then she had already lost sight of him but his footsteps, in the quiet of the night, showed quite clearly where he was going. He headed down the street that led to the Ark, then turned. Noah's wife stopped dead; he was headed for the house where a prostitute lived but then he went straight past it. He leant against a doorway, listened, went onwards, took a few steps to the right, changed his mind, bore left, and Noah's wife heard the dogs leaping up against a fence. Noah seemed to hide under a tree but then could be seen again in the moonlight. He stopped on a terrace looking down at the river and, now and again, he would stretch out his hand, first with the palm upwards, then the back of his hand.

His wife found him sitting beside a trench. He didn't seem surprised or show it in his voice. Noah's wife squatted down next to him and asked what he was looking for. He pointed to the puddle in the trench, 'Groundwater.' Noah's wife agreed that this would cost the builder money, with the cellars always damp like that. But Noah replied that the water wouldn't come from the cellars, it would come in through the doors and leave the house by the chimney. 'The ground has all the water in its belly that will drown it in the end.'

Why was he out at night anyway, Noah's wife chided, he knew how delicate his sinuses could be, he really shouldn't walk about the streets at night. Noah replied, though, that he had not been walking through streets but through canals, and that one day these canals would burst their banks where people see rooftops today. He had been looking to see whether the terraces might serve as tying-up points, but there was no point. Admittedly, you couldn't hear through the doors what was going on in the houses but the doors were certainly not watertight. Frogs croaked. 'Even this croaking is too good for this country, it seems to me I'd begrudge it even the whimper of dogs—drowned, that's how I'd like to see this country.' 'And you tell me this after we've been married thirty years,' said Noah's wife in amazement, then asked why everything had to drown. Noah said, 'I took a good look at society and really had nothing to say but: Let it rain.'

Noah's wife wanted to help her husband without their sons noticing; up until now, if she had ever needed to share her thoughts, she would share them with Noah, and now she looked around to see who else there was. She considered. The timber merchant must be ready to lend an ear, especially now that his daughter and her Japheth were so much together; her worries had to be his worries too. But the timber merchant said that it was an article of faith with him that the customer was always right. Then Noah's wife thought that the lawyer had to be able to persuade Noah, after all, the lawyer was an educated man, a champion of justice. But when she caught up with the lawyer once, on-site, he said regretfully that he was bound to respect his friend's wishes even if he could not always agree with them. Then Noah's wife looked around for someone who didn't need to spare the feelings of customers or friends, and decided to go to the oldest of the priests.

At the portals, she bent low and held out a gold chain. 'For the orphans.' 'For the Orthodox orphans or the others?' asked the oldest priest in a kindly voice. Noah's wife regretted her answer as soon as she said that it was all the same to her, that she had come because something was up with Noah, and they, the holy Fathers that is, had surely been to the building site, it was a hive of activity, well anyway, Noah certainly cared for her, she said, for his wife, but he didn't listen to her, whenever she said anything he just gave her a kiss, but it was different with a priest.

'He chased my colleague away from his site.' The priest pointed to a young man standing there with arms crossed and a piercing gaze, and then added, over his shoulder, 'threatened him with an axe.' 'He doesn't mean anything by it,' said Noah's wife, defending her husband. 'Maybe not,' said the elder, picking up the thread. 'Well, what should we do? If I ever actually met your husband at the services, I might be able to have a word with him.' He weighed the chain in his hand, letting it run through his fingers link by link. 'It's not easy for you. We aren't the only ones who are concerned.' 'But it's not about me,' interrupted Noah's wife. 'An Ark, an Ark,' continued the oldest priest thoughtfully, cleared his throat and rocked his head from side to side, then suddenly he asked, 'What does this Ark mean? So far as we have heard, it's a ship—yes, we know, without sails and without any of the usual equipment.' 'Noah says that wherever he lands is his harbour,' explained Noah's wife, a plea for understanding in her eyes, her mouth drawn tight. 'The sea for this ship has yet to be discovered,' chipped in the young theologian. 'Noah says that it's not a ship that goes to the sea, that the sea will come to it,' Noah's wife explained, and told the two of them what her husband had told her. 'Meso-potamia will become a sea, but when it comes it will be called a deluge.' Her two listeners looked at one another, the elder shut his eyes briefly, lifted his gaze and spoke in a warm, caring tone. 'When you married your husband, you promised to follow him everywhere. He led you to the most splendid house in Mesopotamia. Did you complain then? You follow him now as well, even into the Ark if you must. Think of this Ark as sent by God to test you.'

Once word got out that Noah was building the Ark against a deluge, the people of Mesopotamia were in uproar.

They asked where on earth Noah got the idea that Mesopotamia deserved to drown. They'd thought that the Ark was simply a hobby of his. Everyone knew the caves at Yegerom, built ages ago by a tremendously wealthy man who died before it was all done. That had been a sort of Ark as well, and these days it was a favourite tourist spot for its stairs and pulpits.

But the Ark seemed to be more than a folly: it was an impertinence, an insult, typically inconsiderate from a rich man like Noah who was known to talk like a navvy and could be seen down at his building site every day, behaving as though he'd been born in a barn. Drowning, they said, that might do Noah some good; the more educated classes spoke of a watery grave, finding death in the waves, while most folk spoke of death at the bottom of a barrel and mimed 'glug, glug'.

Now everyone knew that the Church had put out the word that Noah was building the Ark against a flood, and when they all wanted to know what exactly a flood, or even a Flood, was, the Church spoke up again and explained that it was something to do with sin, for we are flawed and at fault, and have fled from God, which is why the Flood would rush down upon Mesopotamia to drown it. Many resisted these 'prophets of the Flood', accusing them of trying to drum up their trade in salvation. In any case, the general conclusion was that it was best to wait and see.

They had all spent some time totting up how often it had rained since work began on the Ark.

Everyone remembered that once there had been such a protracted downpour that work on the Ark had to be interrupted for weeks, and was not resumed when the rain stopped and the water level dropped in the dingles and dells. The site was still under water for a long time and the wood so damp that there was no question of working with it, however much Noah ranted and raved. People remembered all the more clearly because, at the time, an argument had broken out over whether Noah should pay wages for the weeks when no work had been done.

The truly old tales of times gone by, when, once it had rained so hard that the hills shed not just water but great masses of earth, landslips far more dangerous than the rain, and many had died flailing in the mud. Toothless old mouths told horror stories. The old folk argued about exactly how many had died, and the more relatives they could number, the more loudly and insistently they made their case. They hobbled about on sticks to show how they had run away; they yelped and shouted as people had called for help at the time. The old men and women ran their hands through their hair and looked at the young folk with a stubborn pride because they still remembered what a real catastrophe was.

When everyone really started talking about the deluge, though, was when a man suddenly appeared who called himself the 'true Noah'. No one knew where he came from, although, many claimed that he had escaped from prison. His accent revealed nothing of his origins either for he sang his sentences. His short-sighted eyes made his face look strained, expectant and rather stupid; his hands showed no signs of ever having worked. Everyone argued, as well, about how old he was: his hair shone like a boy's but his face could collapse into a mass of wrinkles quite suddenly, and he had a clear double chin. He gave sermons on the building site, until Noah drove away the 'true Noah'. The new arrival, who called himself a 'prophet of the new age', cursed Noah and his wood. He held out his hands and announced that the true Ark was his hands: when it rained, he would fold his hands, and they would grow into a great ship, where any could embark who were ready to atone for their sin and bring offerings. Hardly anyone openly declared their faith in the 'true Noah' but it was common knowledge that there was a black market in tickets for the ship of his hands.

When the police searched the house that some unknown patron had given to the preacher, they found boots and whips; over a dozen women tried to stop the police from entering, shrieking and tearing their hair when the police led the 'true Noah' away; these were single women, many from good families, who had laid their wealth and their savings at the feet of the 'true Noah' and, when he accepted these offerings, were allowed to call themselves 'handmaidens of the New Age'. Word on the street had it that the house was used not for ceremonies and services but for orgies, and one woman had put up a long struggle before she would show the blue bruises on her back. But the police could prove nothing against him. Even when the 'true Noah' was held in a dark cell, in solitary confinement, he denied having held orgies; he cited as proof of his innocence that he was impotent, that Nature had spared him in advance from any sin. In court, he called out to his devotees, telling them that when the time came, his hands would wax strong, he would tear down all bars and break every wall, and then take the faithful aboard his ship and sail with them across drowning Mesopotamia.

General derision gave way to disquiet as the rainy season approached. Prices for millet and flour rose and any attempts at reassurance simply awoke more fear and concern. Many insisted on taking their holidays and spent them up in the hill country where they praised the bracing climate; others went off to the rivers and made friends with the fishermen. When the rains came, the seed germinated, the fields became green, the wells and cisterns filled. It became obvious: there had never been so few cellars flooded—many more people these days lived in good solid houses with stone foundations.

While everyone got back to work, confident and relieved, Noah's sons decided to take action.

Shem was the oldest. As a child he had experienced how all of a sudden there was another child, a child that screamed when he pinched it; he had been beaten for this, and slouched off to throw stones at storks. But by the time his second brother came, Shem was long used to seeing the others carried in his mother's arms while he walked on his own two feet. Certainly, he would give his little brothers a shove when they stood up from a squat, but he was happy too, because they ran with him and watched the frogs that he caught. He didn't just shut his brothers in the barn, he also taught them how to set snares. Later he wrote letters for his brothers to copy; he showed off his pubic hair while they tugged in embarrassment at their downy fluff; he was the first to stay out all night, and since then had always been the oldest brother, the first to have children of his own.

Japheth, the middle son, wore his older brother's clothes until they were worn out; he wished dearly to grow bigger than his brother. Usually the clothes had to be taken in, and the shoes too had usually been mended by the time he got them. Which is why he took no heed of anything, climbed every tree and scrambled over fences, shredding his clothes and himself as well. He always had a scab somewhere and picked or sucked at it in secret. When his older brother wanted to set him to do chores, he fought back; but he brawled not just with the big boy but with the little one too, for he had a younger brother as well. In the end, of course, he did his share, was the only one to rub the camels down, the first to learn to milk. When Shem had misplaced his shirt, their mother called to her middle son, 'Japheth, where is Shem's shirt?' And when Ham, the youngest, was looking for his shoes, their mother asked her middle son, 'Haven't you seen Ham's shoes?' Then the tears would start from Japheth's eyes in anger but she calmed him, saying, 'You've got more sense than them.' However hard he fought this fate, one day Japheth simply gave up and decided to be the sensible one of the three.

Ham, the youngest, was said to be a feast-day child. He had come into the world on a feast day, and he also said of himself that he had been conceived on a feast day, on an afternoon in bed digesting an opulent meal; if there had been any other entertainment on offer that afternoon, he said, then he would never have been born. Which is why it was quite all right that he didn't have to wear old clothes, and he would be happy to teach others the best way to spoil and pamper him. He never got involved in arguments but pushed his brother forwards in his place; he said of himself that he was no good at numbers but had quite a talent for spending and knew just enough of languages to get what he wanted. He combed a cow-lick down onto his forehead, looked upwards at the others with his head cocked to one side and gnawed his lip in finely judged dismay.

Shem, the oldest son, called together his brothers because something had to be done. There had been an argument at the sheep-shearing. Japheth was not just there to make sure that the sheep were held properly between the knees so that the knife didn't hurt them, but he sheared as well, himself—not as quickly as Shem but more carefully than the others. When their father came and asked how much wool they might reckon with, Shem named the price. Noah said that this was good, almost too much for unwashed wool, but he needed the money for the tween decks. Then Shem leapt to his feet; a half-shorn sheep ran, bleating, between father and son. When his father left, Shem clutched at his head, his hands clammy with fury and from the work.

He knew, Shem said, that it was a hard step to take, and he did rather wish that Ham would actually listen. He'd thought it all over but if things went on like this then one day they would find themselves empty-handed. Their mother, who came in by chance, cursed at them; she would never let her husband be declared a legal ward, that kind of thing would be held against their children, his children's children, they would only have to apply for a civil service position and then someone would say, ah yes, their grandfather was non compos. Shem would not be dissuaded, though. He had been to the public library and looked it up in a law book because he mistrusted the lawyer, whom he called a shyster. He produced a sheet of paper and said that it was mistaken to assume that taking a person into ward was intended to harm them; and he read aloud. Guardianship over wards was to be imposed in those circumstances 'when the ward needs constant support from others for his own good and protection'. Shem conceded that their father had not developed vicious habits or brought himself into disrepute but there was an obligation to consider imposing guardianship when, and again he read aloud, 'the estate is held and administered in such a way as to expose the family to the danger of bankruptcy.'

Japheth agreed that something had to be done, seeing as that he was engaged and wanted to marry soon. Ham chortled that if Japheth was going to marry the timber merchant's daughter, then at least part of the lost money would stay in the family. Shem paid no heed to any of this and carried on, saying that he had noticed how their father would suddenly stop in the middle of the street and look for rain in a clear blue sky; above all, it seemed to him that ather was tired, more tired than you would expect from a man of his age, and they needed to go to a doctor rather than a judge. 'Good luck getting him to a doctor,' scoffed Noah's wife. But Japheth explained that this was a modern doctor, you didn't even have to undress for an examination, he simply talked and let you talk in turn. 'Does that help?' asked Noah's wife. They had sent Esther's brother to this doctor, Japheth explained, he'd got into the habit of stealing spoons without needing the money or anything, and the doctor had found out that the boy was not getting enough love at home. 'That can't be anything to do with it,' protested Noah's wife. 'Well, in any case, they love him more at home these days,' insisted Japheth, 'and he's given up stealing spoons.'

Ham hitched up his belt and tugged at the lock of hair that hung down his forehead. 'You've got it easy, my dear brothers both, at least you have your fields and your herds. But me?' He made a wry mouth and licked his lips. 'I've been robbed of my only distinction. I would have become the greatest con man of Mesopotamia but what shall I do now that everyone is living beyond their means? They've stolen my thunder. Yes, if anyone has cause for complaint, it's me. It's me you should be helping, not our father.' He looked at the floor and sketched shapes in the dust with his right shoe. 'I can't do what he wants, though. He always wants to know where I spend my time. But how can I say in advance where I might wake up on any given morning?' Seeing that their mother looked away at this, Ham fell silent, pursed his lips, shrugged his shoulders and leant across to Shem. 'Mind you, it's all become easier. Earlier, I always had to tell the girls, I love you so much. Now, I just whisper in their ear, this might be the last evening before the end. These evenings will sweep me away.'

Their mother protested that for days her husband had not spoken a word, not even poked at his food, ever since he had learnt that she had told the priests he was building the Ark against a Flood. She didn't want to suffer through any more such days. Japheth told Shem to bear in mind that their father had a lawyer on hand who knew all the tricks; for the time being, it was certainly better to rely on a doctor. They agreed to work on their father until he visited the doctor, even just once. They agreed not to be too heavy-handed about it: point out when his palms were sweating, tell him how distracted he seemed, talk about cases of people who had waited too long to ask for help although they could have been cured without further ado.

When Noah was adding the second new storey, Erim the camel-drover still refused to do a hand's turn.

He usually had a drop hanging off the end of his nose that would not fall for an age, since Erim found any kind of movement too much bother; why wipe the drop when it would fall on its own anyway? It was only when the drop began to tickle that he would hawk it back up into his nostrils. When he spat, it was the result of long consideration and practice; he spat like a marksman, not missing a stone, and his showpiece was to spit against the wind.

His wife threatened that she would walk the streets in rags, but Erim, the camel-drover, asked whether in fact she had any clothes but rags, at which his wife burst into tears and sobbed that everyone should see what kind of husband she had. Erim urged her to walk the streets as she threatened, since, then, all would see what kind of wife he had. She wept and blew her nose on her knuckles: 'Everyone makes money on building the Ark but you,' and when he spat past her, aiming at a stone, she blabbered on, 'and not just earned nothing from it but we still owe money for the rent.'

Erim liked to stand around on the site, not to set his hand to any task but to watch the others work. He would shout 'Ho!' when there was no beam laid ready on the ropes, so that the immigrant workers, startled out of their waiting, would heave at their lines and fall flat in the dust. The foreman switched between offering Erim work and having him escorted from the site but Erim would not be chased away. He would stand around at the edge of the site; if the workers looked at him, he would gaze heavenwards and stretch his hand out like Noah, greeting the cloud overhead.

It was Erim who first voiced the suspicion that Noah was mad. He followed Noah everywhere, a few paces behind him so that he could duck back behind a tree or the corner of a house when Noah turned round. If the two of them crossed paths nevertheless, then Erim would stretch out his hand, making Noah laugh, but Erim would say that he wasn't looking for the Flood; rather, he wanted a couple of the drops that clink as they fall, the kind that can be exchanged; he earned nothing from the Ark, he said, he was the beggar they had left at liberty and liberty was expensive; so perhaps Noah could help him finance his life of leisure.

Since Noah was constantly looking up to the skies when he took his walks, he once fell into a well. Erim was the first to call for help and run for a rope. But Erim was also the first to spread the news that Noah did not have enough money on him to reward his rescuers. Others argued with him, saying that rich people didn't need to carry money around with them and could be pulled out of wells even on credit. But Erim also claimed that Noah had fallen into the well deliberately. The draughtsman dismissed this idea with high-handed derision: Why would Noah leap into a cistern to die, when he was all set to save himself from the Flood?

The timber merchant and the draughtsman decided that, being good friends of Noah's, they should go to the lawyer; no one would care to see Noah's reputation at the mercy of a camel-drover, whatever they may think of Noah himself. 'Earlier I used to build kitchen cupboards,' said the timber merchant to open the discussion, 'but did I ask whether people had anything to put inside? What would happen if every time I made a bed, I asked what went on in it?' But the other two didn't rise to his off-colour joke. 'Slander is punishable by a fine,' began the lawyer, 'but since Erim has no money, the fine would be commuted to a prison sentence. Certainly, the sentence isn't so harsh that he would be locked away for long, but I think I know enough of the prison system to say that even a cadaverous camel-drover will come out rather thinner than he went in. The best thing to do would be to have him disappear.' 'That idle layabout,' said the draughtsman in disgust. 'A layabout?' The lawyer's eyes lit up. 'There are provisions for sectioning the work-shy, permanently, if there's good cause.' He slapped the other two on the shoulder. 'In a period of full employment, when we have to import foreigners, here's someone who is not just refusing to contribute his labour to the workforce, he's even interfering with the work of others—a deluge would be just about the thing for spongers like that.'

There was someone else who got by just as she always had but was still waiting impatiently for the deluge.

She hadn't done it for money from the very start but slipped into the habit from one man to the next. It all began with one early affair when pocket money changed hands; her first lover had said to her, on the very first evening, 'Take your silly hands off me,' and then when she got up afterwards, 'You enjoyed it too.' She worked for her next boyfriend, since he was a student who couldn't bear being dependent on his parents. Once he had finished his exams, she met someone who wanted a woman who was merely a woman; she took care of the cooking and cleaning. Then came a lesbian interlude, very relaxed but passionless. From then on, she would accept an invitation to dinner here, an invitation to bed there, let herself be led astray and led them on while she did so and afterwards, least said, soonest mended.

Before the general prosperity, she used to stand in the doorway of the Blue Heaven bar, with the landlord's permission. She wore a dress slit just far enough up the leg to keep the police from taking steps, and would cast her eyes downwards in a way that made even the cop on the beat smile back at her. Since the law didn't allow her to actually speak to anyone, she would ask with her shoulders and call with her breasts and answer with her toes. Once the owner rebuilt the Blue Heaven and had the large mosaic put on the wall with the abstract picture of the two rivers, and once the staff began to bring the wrong drinks or dishes because they didn't speak Mesopotamian all that well, the owner wanted to ban the prostitute from his premises. A lot of men took their wives out for the evening these days and didn't want to meet a tart who would perhaps say hello as they passed. It was made clear to Chlea that she would have to leave the place in the evenings, and he told her of a park along the Euphrates she could use, and she made do with that. 'The highland Turks look like my type, I'll soon stop their singing.'

She lived with an old waiter. He had kept on working even when his hands began to tremble; even though he often slopped and spilled the orders he served, landlords competed to offer him high wages. They used to say that he was the last real waiter left in Mesopotamia. He could read customers and tell what they wanted from their eyes and fingers, but was never pushy about it; he was always polite, regardless of what was ordered, and attentive to the customer's needs but never personal; he would never have seated guests together who were strangers to one another. He asked the guests how they were without wanting to know any more than that. One day, though, he simply quit. The landlord wanted him to take the next order while the glass was only half empty; he spoke up on the guests' behalf but the guests called his name loudly across the room, and when they complained, he realized that they were complaining since they felt like it, rather than because they knew something was wrong.

He brought Chlea her breakfast in bed; he combed his hair while it was still wet so that the strands lay across his bald pate like the teeth of the comb. He waited patiently while Chlea tasted the breakfast. He plumped up her pillow and placed it behind her back. If Chlea wanted a different kind of bread, she would describe what she wanted, coyly admitting that she was a fussy woman but also that she was helpless without a servant. The old waiter himself had no dearer wish than that she would wish for other services. Chlea let him pick out her clothes. They shared the same tastes; muted with one dominant colour. But they also quizzed one another and shot questions back and forth, each wanting to hear what the other thought, wanting to speak their own mind.

The waiter would kiss her when she left the house, in a fatherly fashion and apologize straight away for becoming personal. He didn't let Chlea pay anything for bed and board, for his services; the old waiter said that he was in her debt, that, at his age, he was happy still to have someone who needed him, and he excused himself for the way his hand trembled. When he died, Chlea put on his tombstone the words that he had been wont to whisper now and then: They don't know how to be served any more.

Since then, Chlea spent her afternoons at the Blue Heaven again, where workers sat and shirked their jobs on the Ark. They scoffed at threats that they would be fired; just let them try taking us off the payroll, they said, while the highland Turks are taking our women and our jobs anyway. When the foreman appeared, they would drink up at their leisure, put on their toolbelts with great ceremony and look to see where the sun stood in the sky. Chlea sat with them, mocked by the old workers, admired by the apprentices and grudgingly tolerated by the landlord. She egged the workers on; get back on-site, she told them, finish the Ark, and then the end could begin.

'And you?' the workers asked, laughing, 'won't you drown too?' 'Of course,' Chlea replied prophetically. 'But only after you. I'll wait until the last man is under water. What use am I without you? Then you'll have to shut shop for good and all,' she teased the landlord. She jumped to her feet and climbed the chair, turned round once, shimmied and thrust up her breasts. 'You lot have no idea what the deluge is.' 'Tell us!' they all called out, while only the landlord lifted his head from the glasses and looked on reproachfully. 'Can I say it so simply that even the last of you pricks can follow me?' Chlea mused aloud and poked out her tongue. 'Right,' she said, 'but the underage have to put their hands over their ears. It's indecent, the deluge. Not for everyone. It needs more from you than wide-eyed innocence. So then, just imagine that heaven has got the hots for the earth, and not just evenings either; the heaven lies atop the earth night and day but there's such a distance between them. If you lot think that heaven and earth get jiggy right now, at the horizon, then go and have a look—you'll find that they're as far apart there as they are over here. Now you know for yourselves that when you're horny you can lose control, so one day heaven will just hurl himself at the earth and then the sparks will really start to fly, and your linen sheets are nothing compared to the clouds, and then when heaven comes, it's just like with you— millions all squirted out for nothing, at the end of the day, only one left alive.'

Chlea slapped her belly. 'That's the good old Ark.' The workers stomped and slapped their thighs. 'You're all cripples,' she shouted into the room, 'Each of you with two heads. Do you know how stupid it looks?' She put a hand above her eyes and peered into the corner, her shoulders hunched. 'Aha! the gentlemen from the vice squad are already on their way. My dear chaps, you're swimming in the wrong direction, eternity is that way. Do you have your papers on you?' She pulled up her dress. 'Higher, higher!' the rest of them shouted, and even those who had been playing backgammon in the corner looked up at Chlea's legs. 'No one here gets out alive. I'm not listening. The storm has spoilt all my fun. Gasp your last, once more, please; not to worry, you're not alone, your family will be along soon. Why go home? House and home are floating away as well. A branch isn't all you need.' She kicked at the table in front of her, beer mugs and glasses shattered on the floor. The landlord came across cursing and swearing, a cloth in his hand. 'She's getting everything soaked.' And as he wiped up, Chlea jumped down from the chair, saying, 'I wouldn't want to be a human in that knocking shop.'

Noah, though, wanted to keep the peace in his household and agreed to be examined.

Noah's wife, accompanied by Japheth, spoke to the doctor beforehand. He smiled and cleaned the lenses of his glasses, saying, 'Very few of my patients even know that they're being treated.' Noah's wife insisted again that Noah must not know that he was sick and must not know that this was an examination; the lawyer had come to see her as well, saying that there was already enough talk about her husband. She had no idea, she said, when it had all begun, if only it were the sort of sickness that they could conceal, but the Ark, that could be seen from everywhere.

The doctor led the two of them to look at a diploma. 'I studied internal medicine. Quite possible that a human being can die because of an intestine or a liver or something else in his innards. I wasn't satisfied knowing this, though.' He went on to the next diploma. 'Pathology, that's where you really know what killed a person. When everyone else in the hospital had failed, and all there was left was a corpse, then my esteemed teacher would come along, an elegant man he was, and make a diagnosis;

and he was always right, since he worked with dead patients. Then I got to thinking, well, what's really worth knowing is why people don't die—now then, what seems to be the trouble with Noah?' the doctor asked suddenly, pulling his white coat together over his stooped shoulders.

The doctor wanted to know what sicknesses Noah had suffered from as a child; he had a form in front of him that he filled in as they went. But Noah's wife said that she had only met her husband very much later. The doctor enquired as to whether there were similar cases in the family. Noah's wife couldn't think of any but Japheth said, 'An aunt . . .' 'A very distant aunt,' said Noah's wife, dismissively. 'And what about this aunt?' asked the doctor, unperturbed. Well, Japheth recounted, one day this aunt had climbed up a tree and never came down again; she hauled her food up on a rope in a basket. The doctor asked what she did when she was up the tree. 'She had them bring her cages and she'd lock away all the birds she caught,' said Japheth, finishing the story.

When Noah came into the consulting room, the first thing he did was rush to the window; he tore aside the curtain and threw open the shutters. A well-aimed sunbeam burst into the room. Noah leant against the wall, smiling, and brought his breathing back to normal. 'I thought the sun had gone down.' The doctor reassured him, closed the shutters again and drew the curtains. 'I like to work in the dark.' Then he held out his hand to Noah, who twitched. 'Are we shaking hands or are you taking my pulse?' he asked. 'My arm hurts,' said Noah to start things out, and then straight away added an explanation, 'that's from always holding it out so straight.' 'Other than that?' asked the doctor, allowing his patient to make the first diagnosis. 'My eyes ache,' Noah admitted. The doctor held up his fingers and asked Noah to watch them very carefully and tested his pupil reflexes; he suggested that he could prescribe a salve, Noah's ache came from looking too much at the sun.

The doctor led Noah to a couch and asked him to sit. Noah let himself be lain down flat. Everything was light and easy, the doctor said, and Noah raised his head for a moment when he heard the doctor say 'relax'—a word he had never heard before. Just forget everything, the doctor said slowly, of course all our troubles will be back next day, but for the time being, it should all just sink away, down into a deep sea—'No!' shouted Noah, sitting up with a start, but he lay down again, settled into the cushion that the

doctor had ready for him, and closed his eyes. Light
and easy, the doctor whispered, light as a little bird.
The doctor stretched out his arms and balanced
them like wings. 'Up, up and away, far away and far
from here.' He looked at Noah's eyelids, shut. 'More
little birds,' spoke the doctor, 'taking you off and
away,' and he listened to Noah's breathing. When the
doctor went to sit down behind Noah though, he sat
up again. He rubbed his forehead and looked at his
hand. 'Not the sea, that's my own sweat,' and then
clung to the couch. 'Wooden, yes, but this is no Ark.'

Noah apologized for having nodded off. The
doctor reassured him though: No one ever gets
enough rest. Time now to talk about something else,
something that had nothing to do with the case. The
doctor spoke about how, when he was young, he had
dreamt of becoming an actor; how he had gone to
the theatre in those days; even during his engage-
ment he never missed a performance, had often
worked as an extra, once he had even been given a
line, but in the end it's better to be an old doctor
than an old actor. And how about Noah, did he like
the theatre, what would be his favourite role, was
there one that he would play if he could? Noah
didn't understand at first; when the doctor repeated
the question, what would Noah most like to play on

stage, Noah thought for a moment and then pointed at himself.

The doctor stretched out his hand invitingly. Should they play flood then, he asked, they were alone, after all, and he wanted to know whether it was an entertaining piece. 'There's one who laughs,' said Noah, and when the doctor then asked when and where the play might be seen, Noah said, 'Soon enough, everywhere.' Noah went on to say that he would need a roof and a tree for his set; not a roof above him though, but beneath him, and not a tree where birds nest but one where fishes spawn. What costume would he wear, asked the doctor. Noah looked down at himself, then drew up a sleeve and showed the flesh of his arm. 'I'll wear my skin, since I can save it.' 'And the Ark is your prop?' enquired the doctor. 'And no audience,' Noah went on, 'since everyone has a part to play, and even if every eye is open at the end, they'll see nothing, not one of them. Oh, the third day,' Noah shouted. 'Stage fright?' asked the doctor, insistently. 'On the third day, the sea will belch back what it swallowed, a raft of corpses, jetsam with no beach to wash up on.' 'And how did Noah come up with this scene?' asked the doctor. 'Ha!' said Noah. He went to the curtain, drew it aside and threw the shutters wide. 'I see land.' He grabbed at the sunbeam and rubbed it between his fingers—'A rainbow!' Then he spun around and said in a flat voice, 'That's the part I'd like to play—getting away safely—and I have one big entrance in the whole piece—when my stage is dry land underfoot.'

The Ark had been begun as a private enterprise but was becoming, more and more, a matter of public interest.

'The Ark is heresy built in wood,' said the young priest to open proceedings, 'visible from far off. There can only be one punishment: burn the heretic since the pyre is already there—the Ark.' He stopped and pushed back his broad sleeves to cross his arms. 'Gently now,' said the oldest priest, since the trade unions leader had indicated that he wanted to speak. 'No one should be surprised that we take up this particular case,' said the young priest emphatically, and looked up at the ceiling and smiled suddenly, 'we are the specialists when it comes to Heaven and we will defend Heaven even against Noah.' 'I'd like to have it on record,' said the trade union leader, 'that I'm not here to learn or argue about private matters, matters such as God or Heaven.' 'Or drowning, singly and collectively,' said the young priest, picking up the trade unionist's thread. 'What a blasphemous thought; the very idea demands punishment.'

'Perhaps God rather overtaxed his strength with Creation,' the union man shot back and planted both his elbows on the table, 'but what if he actually does let it rain?' 'In that case,' said the young priest, looking briefly at his interlocutor and then answering into empty air, 'I will drown to prove God wrong and my theology right.'

'We came here for a preliminary discussion,' chided the oldest priest, 'we already know what we disagree on but we would like to discover what, if anything, can bring us together in considering the Ark.' 'Father,' his young colleague bowed his head to the chairman, 'pardon my excitement. What a laughable superstition though, it's like something the peasants would believe.' 'The landowners believe worse,' the trade unionist threw in. 'He hasn't the imagination to think of more than the weather,' continued the young priest, 'what a superficial view he has of the Flood! If God destroys the world, he destroys himself; the deluge is ruled out on theological grounds alone.' The trade unionist drummed a rhythm on the tabletop but the other man paid no attention. 'Father, you know what kind of life I led before I began to study God's works.' The chairman waved this away. 'I am talking about a deluge that happens every day, that need not even dampen our eyes. What matter if dams burst in the mountains or breakwaters in the ports; there is a dam that bursts in our bosom. This is the disaster that I have seen, and every day a miracle too; we come through it all.'

'I can hardly blame Noah if he struggles with how things are,' said the trade unionist into the pause. He asked that they not interrupt him; he emphasized what it meant that he was even ready to come to this meeting, and saying so cast his eyes around the hall, looking at the candlesticks and scrolls, smiling faintly. 'Youthful memories.' He carried on in a more serious tone; they would understand, of course, that he was speaking only for himself but the thing was that he just couldn't understand why the Church was getting so wound up about Noah; after all, the temples had been empty long before this whole business began; whatever you might care to accuse Noah of, could be refuted by just taking a stroll through the streets of Mesopotamia. With Noah, you had to draw the line between what he thought he was doing and the actual outcome; being a no-nonsense sort of chap himself, he could only see the effects that Noah was having.

'The Flood as a solution to our social problems,' said the young priest scornfully, 'it's a miracle that no one had the idea before now. You're forgetting, my respected friend, that the lower classes will drown as well.' 'Noah is exaggerating,' smiled the trade unionist, 'there have always been rich folk but never one with such a bad conscience.' 'In any case, he did as you wished and he's one of yours now,' said the young priest bitterly. 'You want to make Noah the Left's business?' asked the politician in surprise. 'Noah? First of all, he was never a card-carrying member. He wants to preserve Creation—is that progressive? Anyone building an Ark has a very poor grasp of revolutionary thought.' 'Anyone preaching universal destruction should be counted on your side,' and the young priest looked at the chairman and threw up his hands so that his sleeves fluttered downwards, and he shook his head at the thought that Noah might be counted as a conservative. 'But I understand why you're shocked. You'd have liked to drown one particular class but now you see that you won't even have the chance to dig society's grave, since the grave-diggers will meet their Maker too.'

The chairman got up from his seat, his right hand on the small of his back, gathered his kaftan in folds about him and set one venerable foot in front of the other; he waved away the stick that the young priest offered him and took the trade unionist's elbow. 'How blue the sky is,' he said reverently at the window, 'an innocent blue. How fortunate that we basically understand one another. We are perhaps closer than our words may reveal. We do not wish to dispute that Noah has now become a useful citizen, any more than that we would dispute the fact that he has become dangerous—unwittingly useful and unwillingly dangerous. You, my young friend, penitent as you are and submissive to God's will, and you, sir, a man of action and a politician—what d'you both make of a man who says that the only solution for our society is for the rain to fall? We may cite this sky as our argument. Noah will drown in his own ridi-cule, he will have his Flood and he will be astonished at how blue and warm it is.'

Though the meeting took place in strict secrecy, the Centre parties learnt of it; word got out that the Orthodox clerics and the Left had dickered over Noah's fate, and it was whispered that the trade unions had intervened at the last moment to prevent the priests from taking action, and at the same time that the Left was putting out feelers to the Church. At this, the lawyer who had drawn up all of Noah's contracts called a meeting of all like-minded people and party members. Before this, though, he went to see the psychiatrist who had drawn up many an expert witness statement for him already; in confidence, of course, but as a representative of the law and a member of the moderate majority, he couldn't afford to be left in doubt in such matters, he would, of course, not reveal what was said and certainly not reveal his sources but it was important for deciding their future and, indeed, current course of action that he should know how Noah actually was; he would be grateful for whatever the doctor could tell him, for the truth, whatever that might be.

Although he had some reservations, the doctor was ready to tell what he knew, considering the way that they had worked together in the past and, he hoped, would do so in future; but this could only be a conversation, nothing in writing. He could reach no immediate conclusion as to Noah's state of health, it was certainly a suitable case for treatment but he doubted that there could be any scientifically un-ambiguous diagnosis; Noah, being a pyknic type, had a noticeably nervous glance. As always, the task here was to go back to the patient's childhood, and here he could confidently say one thing at least, that given his exaggerated fear of water, Noah must have been a great bedwetter as a child—the experience had left him with a disproportionate guilt complex; there seemed to be no information at all about Noah's father, and it was unclear . . . here the lawyer interrupted him, 'Guilt complex, guilt complex, I really don't understand, he had everything he might wish for.' 'This society makes him suffer,' explained the doctor. 'I'd just like to know whether it's anything serious,' said the lawyer, repeating his question. 'From a human or a medical point of view, hardly,' declared the doctor, 'I'd like to know more but when I met Noah on the street and asked if I should be seeing him again, he said, if I can be helped, then the whole thing's lost.'

Street traders and shopkeepers came to the meeting, tradesmen and primary teachers, farmers and civil servants, money-changers and mid-ranking officers. This was a meeting of the Centre which claimed to be the voice of reason, the moderates, the golden mean. The lawyer stood on the little stage and thanked everyone for giving up their evening to come; he said that he did not want to take up much of their time but that everyone sitting here had heard the rumours that were flying around; it was a serious moment and thus a moment for responsible folk, meaning a moment for the moderates. Live and let live had been their forefathers' motto, and surely there couldn't be so many different kinds of truth that new truths were always waiting to be discovered—coin is coin, unless the counterfeiters are at work. They were never the ones to enquire into a man's faith and the prayers he said, they thought it rather fine that there were people who believed and prayed; nor have our highland Turks ever been cause for concern, even though they had strange customs, surely one could agree on that. Society has no right to intervene until someone becomes a danger to the community as a whole. But when there were wheels within wheels, the lawyer said, when there were cliques and cosy little arrangements—'I'm naming no names here,' said the lawyer, raising his voice, 'since we're on the side of the victims, as we always have been, which is why we are, and now I do name a name, on Noah's side, tomorrow, yesterday, today—since, in our society, everyone has the inalienable right to believe that the end is nigh.'

Why should the end be nigh, they said in Mesopotamia, when we are men of goodwill.

The police had goodwill towards everyone not a uniformed officer, meaning the majority; the police had become everyone's friend and helper. If a child was crying on the street, lost and lonely, the policeman took him by the hand and led him to the station, and every police station had a stock of toys ready and waiting. Police officers carried shopping bags for old ladies. Police officers had been briefed to offer a detainee a cup of warm milk before the interrogation; use of the truncheon was reserved for serious situations and putting the boot in had been banned entirely. Only higher-ranking officers were allowed to use a detained suspect's first name in addressing him. The police took courses not just in self-defence but also in etiquette; they learnt not just how to land a karate chop but also how to smile. The Chief Constable had introduced this initiative 'in order to create a straightforward relationship of trust between the population and law enforcement which had previously been disturbed by misplaced zeal and regrettable incidents.'

But there were too few police officers, even though it was common knowledge that policing was a job with a future. Because there was full employment, hardly anyone applied to work in the public sector any more, since it was so poorly paid compared to equivalent private sector work; nevertheless, the police were lucky that they kept alive a sense of honour and duty unrivalled elsewhere. Be that as it may, the Chief Constable made an appeal to the general public: the job now was to create a voluntary special constabulary where no one should think himself too lowly to play a part, a police force with no uniform, a police force equipped with neighbourly love, a watchful eye and an open ear; a little vigilance here and a word in the right place there, and a major infraction could be nipped in the bud and a crime prevented. 'Be of goodwill towards one another,' the Chief Constable told the public, 'keep an eye out for one another.'

If there was straw piled up in front of a house, someone would come and clear it away, though it posed no danger to him personally; it was well known that flammables lying around like this could easily tempt folk to arson who might never have thought before of setting a fire. If, one morning, a window stayed shut in a house or a flat, the neighbours would be round before midday, knocking at the door, since you never knew what might have happened in the night. If an adult saw another grown-up talking to a child on the street, then he would take up position next to the child and tell the other fellow the way or answer whatever his question was. You couldn't always see the faces at the window, keeping an eye on who came and went or who walked on past but, if you were sharp-eyed yourself, you could see the curtains moving even without a wind. They also kept an eye on people's expenditures, and if someone was spending a lot then they would do their sums; many a thief had been nabbed because he gave himself away by spending too freely. If a man was paying court to a widow, she would soon enough hear from well-intentioned people whether her suitor really was due to come into some money as he claimed. The police were most grateful and followed up every report; any suspicion might be a solid lead, and it was better to end up on a wild goose chase than to suddenly come across a real murder victim. There was only one report that the police never took seriously since they heard it so often: that Noah had been seen walking the streets alone at night, squatting down on others' building sites and peering into the trenches.

Yes, they had goodwill towards one another, and goodwill towards the children too. All parents had long ago been taught not to hit their children if they stuck out their tongue or failed to come into the house the first time they were called. Children, you see, have strange and hidden reasons for doing what they do, which we must seek and find out. No teacher these days would force a left-handed child to use his right hand for the spoon for they did not want to stifle the developing personality; and even if a child broke the crockery, seemingly out of sheer wilfulness, no one would raise their voice, everyone realized that the child simply wanted to draw attention to himself. Goodwill was there in abundance for the next generation, at least more than those who were now the fathers and mothers had ever enjoyed.

And the genders too had goodwill for one another. Many a boy came to know woman before he had learnt to pleasure himself with his hands, and many were already bored with women at an age when, for their fathers, women had only just begun to be more than a dream. It was said that suppressing these urges was bad, long experience having taught where that would lead. They made their own discoveries, not without embarrassment at first, while they were young, but soon enough with a free and easy expertise in hooking up and breaking up. Seduction itself was not a problem, rather the question of where two people could be alone for half an hour or more. The classic women's honeymoon sickness, cystitis, was hardly diagnosed these days; couples had ordinarily taken their honeymoon before marriage, so to speak, so that the wife no longer spent the nights after the wedding with the bedclothes thrown aside.

Goodwill between the genders was also shown in how they looked evermore alike. The young men let their hair grow long, put it in curlers or had it permed; according to surveys, the idea that a crew cut was masculine was simply a prejudice of their parents' generation. When a lad with a fashionable haircut went for a walk with a girl, from a distance they looked like two sisters out for a stroll. On the other side of the coin, there were girls who had crew cuts; if they wanted something, they would whistle for it, and they said hello with their elbows. Distinguishing all too strictly between the genders had long fallen out of fashion.

There was goodwill too for the pederasts. They were the last to wear the traditional grey suits of Mesopotamian menfolk. They didn't want to draw attention to themselves, and thus drew attention by dressing in such a sober and masculine fashion. Pink and violet had long become chic even for the macho type. Many a young man who had had his fill of women was looking around for the next thrill; many another man who had had his doubts earlier in life and had married to fit in, now gave way to his orientation; in an office romance, it was surprisingly easy to hop from a woman's bed to a man's, so that even the most optimistic social reformers were taken aback; and many a teenager who felt that his parents short-changed him on pocket money was happy to earn a little on the side. Maybe not the sort of fun he'd have chosen for himself but fun nevertheless. The pederasts scratched their brows with manicured nails at the sight of a broad-chested workman's nipples, and tittered in delight at the choice on offer. More from habit than necessity, they still frequented those dimly lit bars whose addresses by now were widely known, although still only whispered. When straight couples went off for a weekend at the riverside, the gay couples would choose the other river, and the pickup line for young men these days was, 'Do you bathe in the Tigris or Euphrates?'

Yes, there was goodwill for all. Experiments on mice had found a way for male mice to indulge their drives without producing young; science then produced an extract that could be taken with water. Many women refused for a long time; but it soon became clear to all that abortion was hardly the answer, needing all those forms and signatures and still carrying some risk despite medical progress. Even the fundamentalists were persuaded that pleasure need not always carry its price. Thus the women agreed to subject themselves to a permanent false pregnancy. There was so much goodwill around that they helped one another ensure that there were not too many Mesopotamians.

Why should the end be nigh, they said, now that everything has changed?

Few people remembered how Mesopotamia had looked before. And even those who remembered, argued. Little children pestered their grandparents with questions, 'How did it look before?' Many a fairy tale began with the phrase, 'Once upon a time there was a tumbledown house in a half-abandoned street.' Anyone asking for an address would hear the answer, 'Do you know the trench dug by the new eight-storey block? Turn right there, go along the street that's being widened, then turn again where it's fenced off, used to be a private park, then you'll soon see the scaffolding.' People had long become used to taking not the shortest route but the one that wasn't blocked off.

Grandmothers had even more questions than their grandchildren. As young wives, they had thrown out pots, lamps and carpets; newly wed, they didn't want the old stuff cluttering up the place, and their own mothers and grandmothers had scolded them for their spendthrift ways, saying that a dish could be kept and used even if it had a crack, and a glass could serve its purpose even if the stem was chipped. When these women went out these days, they could see in the shop windows those same pots, lamps and dishes that they had long ago thrown out; and when they went to visit the young folk, they were surprised to find the carpets that they had put away in the attic no longer laid on the floors but hung on the walls and framed. So the grandmothers told their daughters and daughters-in-law not to throw anything away; you never knew whether today's kitchenware might be tomorrow's work of art.

The young people paid more for an old wardrobe than for a new one, even if the doors no longer opened. They went into ecstasies over stools that no one could sit on because they were riddled with worms. Any modern household worth the name had to have something from the olden days next to its modern furniture—whether old door knockers or threadbare horse blankets; the most popular pieces were drinking canteens such as the shepherds used, which could be found with richly coloured ornamentations. Dealers made tours of Mesopotamia, visiting the backwood areas and knocking on the doors of lonely houses; they would hold out bundles of banknotes to whoever answered the door, usually a widow, and asked to be allowed to take a little look around, talking all the while of how impractical this old lumber was, and that people had a right to some comfort in their old age, happy to take away whole doors and window grilles; there was a huge demand for everything that had outlasted a generation.

The change took place in front of everyone's very eyes, and still they were amazed when they went up to the hills on bank holidays to take in the view of Mesopotamia. They looked for the house where they lived among all the new-builds. The larger towns grew every time you went out for a stroll; it became harder to tell one small town from another, since they grew together and merged, and the houses encroached from all sides on the site of the Ark. People pointed at the great square blocks, not so large as the Ark but so much better suited to the landscape, being designed for it. There was the prison, no inmates yet, with its two impressive wings, the men's prison and the women's, and a huge tower for the guards, no longer with a small courtyard for the half hour's exercise each day but a spacious green park; a hedge of laurel, tall as a child, was planted along the inside of the prison wall so that it looked a little friendlier for the inmates. And people pointed out the new hospital and the plot that had been staked out for the cemetery; never in Mesopotamia's history had such care been taken for the dead to come.

Yes, everything had changed, including the festivals. The most important, most popular and most funfilled was the Barefoot Festival, when everyone went barefoot in memory of the times when only a few could afford sandals; they wore rags and draped tatters artfully about themselves. Ambitious revellers worked on their paupers' costumes for months in advance, since the most impressive get-up won a prize. They took to the streets in groups, starting early and going on to the next morning. They could stop at any house they chose and beg for a bowl of soup, and some houses had a constant stream of visitors. The costumed groups had to sing, though, wheedling songs which they howled and groaned so that the barking dogs at the fences slunk back into their kennels. The streets were noisy with woeful dirges and with laughter or cheerful applause from the windows, and if two groups crossed paths they competed as to who could groan the loudest. For Barefoot, bakers baked crispy little rolls for the day's fun, no bigger than a mouthful, called hunger-bread, and many festival-goers sewed them onto their rags and tatters like buttons.

Parties and festivals had all become quite different, and so had art. No artist had starved in a damp garret for a long time now to be able to afford brushes and pigments, or died in obscurity. All new houses were built with large, white walls; people were hungry for decoration and chose art for preference. State buildings were also beautified with room for sculptures in their wide lobbies and foyers, and numerous fountains needing an artwork were opened up for competition. Many in the crafts and skilled trades changed jobs and became artists instead, and many an artist worked day and night. One day, though, most of these artists were simply tired out, never wanting to see a paintbrush or chisel again in their lives, and shut themselves away, watching the market in their rough sketches and preparatory studies grow, the prices for their works rise.

Art these days had much more variety than before. Sculptors went out into the countryside looking for roots to display on their plinths; one artist no longer painted his canvas but took a knife to it, and there was general adulation for the way he placed the slits. Others painted with their eyes closed, to be able to express themselves more immediately they explained, and others again used their models as paintbrushes, rolling them over the canvas. When a new name was mentioned, the immediate question was, 'What's his new thing?' There were also dealers offering variety, shopkeepers who sold not fruit and vegetables, shoes or fabric but art. From time to time, the artists would exhibit their newest works in these shops, and every such occasion was marked by a little vernissage, and if you were invited to these parties then you'd arrived. Never before had art developed so quickly, been left behind so quickly; everything changed so fast that anything that aimed to be more than a sketch seemed in poor taste.

The poets too said that they were the expression of the boom times—the building and tearing down; their place in society had changed entirely. A government office had calculated the percentage of how much creative talent might be expected in a population, on average, and a sum of money was earmarked to cater for this percentage—the money paid out to poets was called grants, and they received awards; there were also numerous forms of encouragement for rising poets and writers. Along with this state subsidy, there were foundations set up with money from the trades. The butchers were the first to give a prize for the most beautiful poem of the year. The jokes about poets finally bringing home the bacon soon fell quiet once the annual amount of money up for grabs became known. But other trades and guilds competed with this prize, there were soon prizes for the best poem of the month, and once there were so many prizes that there were hardly any works left to receive them, the prizes were given as grants in advance and as writing fellowships for works which had not yet been written.

A very famous writer was Jon's son, who no longer wrote 'It was Wednesday morning' but 'It was when? The morning, When's Day.' He had great success reading to packed houses, rarely looking up from his book except once in a while to let the audiences know how much he despised them. Here was a writer who said straight out that prosperity kills, that when society is fat and overripe then the belly fills up the space where the brain should be, that they were all numbed by the good life, jaded and replete, and that if the deluge came then it would be a flood of vomit.

His poetic counterpart was a delicate young man who had adopted a foreign-sounding name. He would smilingly say that poets had always acted as a counterweight; that in a society that sweats and toils, there has to be someone who belongs to the realm of dreams, who speaks with the clouds, to whom the flowers entrust their beauty. Thanks to the subsidies, he had not just the flat where he lived with his family but also another where he wrote his poems and kept his mistress. He was working on a book which had already gone through several titles—he said that the secret is robed in shifting change, that he sang of the air, he sang of the walls, he sang of night and of her hair. He would leap to his feet in the middle of an evening's entertainment, look abstractedly at the people around him, scribble lines in the air with his right hand and excuse himself; there was a poem come upon him, he had to write. Those left sitting behind would argue over who had the right to pay his tab.

Noah, though, did nothing for art and bought no artworks for his Ark, but he was no longer considered benighted since he was at least a patron of science.

At first, Noah had turned for help to an old teacher who had left behind the schoolroom. He knew him from the days when the teacher had often asked Noah to come to see him because of Ham's bad marks and poor behaviour; Noah never went across to the school building so the teacher came to see him in the evenings. These regular visits led to a kind of friendship that gave Noah the courage to ask, since the teacher had hung up his gown, whether he would have time now for a commission. The teacher, though, said that he was an old man and he had found his life's work: a pond. It may be only a little corner of Mesopotamia, he said, but wonders can

often be found near at hand in the most familiar sur-
roundings. Even while he was a teacher he had visited the pond, year after year, with the sixth form,
and had them write about all the insects, amphibians
and birds that could be found in and around this
pond. Now that he was in the twilight of his years,
he went on, he was collecting everything that he had
seen, and that was his world now; if Noah was serious about this commission, then he should get in
touch with the National Institute.

When Noah set foot inside the National Institute, the students swarmed about him. The Director
of the Institute bowed deeply in greeting, which
embarrassed Noah so much that he stepped back
in surprise, knocking over a skeleton. None of the
students dared laugh as the skull rolled across the
floor and Noah went after it on all fours; the spine
sprang apart into its constituent vertebrae, and Noah
grabbed left and right, gathered up a pile of bones,
held a forearm in his hand and tried to fit it into an
ankle. The Director gestured and the students took
the bones from his hand and helped him to his feet.
Noah was amazed at how expertly the students
put the bones back together, and he smiled as the
reassembled bones came to look more and more like
a human skeleton.

The director led Noah through the halls. Behind every student stood another waiting to take his place, while those who were busy examining specimens, explained what they saw to other students peering over their shoulders. The Institute Director told Noah that it was an honour to have him visit. Noah was looking at the door and listening with only half an ear as the Director complained, 'Mesopotamia can find the money to build roads but none for this Institute.' The Director caught up with Noah at the door but Noah pulled him outside and explained why he had come; he wanted a list of all the animals, a catalogue of everything alive.

Immediately a scientific row broke out over where life began. Noah had been quite clear in his wishes that he wanted a list of everything that lived; the bone of contention was about whether viruses should be counted as living beings, those tiny packets of protein that can cause, for instance, foot and mouth disease or rabies, whether they should be included. In the end, though, this argument was confined to specialists, and, since the commission was enough to keep all scientists busy, the disputing parties agreed not to include viruses in the list but to write a special monograph for Noah, to explain to him that, although the Institute accepted the commission in good faith, it was no easy matter to decide where life begins.

The Institute expanded. Noah had declared that he was ready to pay the donation they asked. In the new halls, almost every student had his own workstation. All the animals of Creation were assiduously described, all the variant names that an animal might bear in different regions were recorded, their feeding habits and breeding seasons noted; Noah was startled to hear how many years it would take until the work was ready but they assured him that it would become a standard work and bear his name as donor and patron. Noah had already found out when work begun on the Ark that everything can take very much longer than planned, and he was glad that he hadn't waited any longer to get started. But when the Director of the Institute (by now the Director Emeritus) and his successor came to deliver the *Codex Noahensis*, it wasn't just the two of them who came but a retinue of servants who carried books and scrolls into Noah's house for hours so that Noah had to clear out his biggest room.

Noah sat in front of the books, gazing in bewilderment at the scrolls on the floor. He waited for an age before opening the first volume. As he leafed through it, his wife came in, clapped her hands together and asked, 'When were you ever interested in books, Noah?' He answered her in a whisper, anxious and lost in thought, 'It's for the Ark.' His wife took her husband's arm. 'You never built the Ark to be a library, did you?' 'No', said Noah. 'I built it for what's in these books,' and he turned a page. Noah's wife began to leaf through one. 'Animals, nothing but animals—but the Ark's too small for all this, by the time we bring all our camels and sheep aboard, and you're taking the goats along, aren't you?' 'We'll take three pairs of those,' Noah told her. 'When our sons hear about this . . .' Noah's wife put in. Then Noah got up, leaning on a table, and suddenly swept the books away with both arms, threw one more onto the pile on the floor, kicked at the scrolls and shouted, 'These beasts, these brutes!' 'Noah,' said his wife, coming to her husband's side, 'I know that you don't talk to me any longer, ever since I told the priests that you're building the Ark against the deluge. But, Noah,' she stroked his hair but took her hand away as soon as she saw how he flinched at the show of affection. She wanted to leave the room but Noah held her back, grabbed her hand but didn't look at her; his wife smiled. 'Now you're acting like one of our boys—they never knew how to start when there was something they wanted to talk about.' 'Is this what life's about, what we're doing?' Noah asked. 'When I was young, I thought that I had to grow up, to be grown up, I thought that's what life is, that's when I decide what I do. And then as I grew I didn't know whether you're a grown-up at fifteen or twenty or later but I realized I have to be older than this. I said to myself, I'll wait until I've had a woman. Then I had women, and met you and stayed with you. I loved you but I would lie awake and think: This is all very well but it can't be everything. I decided: When I'm a father then I'll really be living the life. I didn't know what to expect but I waited and was sure that something or other would happen. Everything I wanted came to me, and if I wanted more I made it come. One more harvest and one more year, empty the barns and fill them again, bring the animals to breed and raise the young to slaughter. Will I have lived by the time I'm lying on my deathbed? Life must be somewhere. Perhaps the mouse is smarter than us, since it never learnt to talk. Maybe life is crouched inside the camel's hump and looks as daft as that just so no one can guess its hiding place. Is life in the bee's sting or in the elephant? I'm taking the elephant along but also the fly that blinds it. Since life isn't in me, it must be elsewhere because I want there to be some life somewhere.'

Noah almost didn't let the naturalist in to see him. When he knocked, Noah was kneeling in front of his scrolls, laughing; he had just found one which listed nothing but fish. 'I'll put that one aside.' He was looking around for other scrolls with only the names of animals that lived in the water, and with every scroll he set aside the happier he became in his search. His wife repeated that a naturalist wanted to talk to him, 'about the animals.' Noah waved her away; only the other day he had chased off a taxidermist who had shown him stuffed gazelles and wild boar, treated with the latest techniques so that they didn't smell and could be placed on show anywhere in a home. 'No more visits about the animals,' Noah snapped. But the naturalist was already inside. He murmured an apology, threw his cape back over his shoulder, an expensive piece of fabric. 'I am rather too elegantly dressed for a scientist,' he said self-deprecatingly, 'but I am a private scholar. Allow me.' He knelt, leafed through the books, drawing his shoulders up and stooping to see; he declared in mock astonishment, 'Just as I thought, alphabetical, the whole of Creation. What a farrago.' At that, Noah asked him to take a seat.

'The whole structure is rather better planned than has previously been assumed,' began the naturalist, crossing his legs and wagging his free foot from side to side as he spoke. 'I have brought along a scroll.' He drew out the scroll, held it in his hand, offering it to Noah but without insisting, a questioning smile on his lips to ask whether he should hand it across. 'I have made a digest, as it were, of all Creation,' he began again and put the scroll on the table next to Noah. 'I have considered every species, examined every genus, left out no family and ignored no intermediary group. I have taken the more unusual creatures into account. Believe me, Noah, this is a representative sample. Of course, there were occasions when I hesitated. There are, after all, animals quite unnecessary for reconstructing biodiversity which are nevertheless very beautiful. Which is how the peacock ended up on the list.'

Noah reached for the scroll but jerked his hand back at the last moment and crossed his arms. 'What about the animals you didn't include?' The scholar nodded. 'I had been expecting your question, it's an obvious one. From what is listed here,' pointing to the scroll, 'you can derive all the rest, generation by generation, of course, and under certain conditions. Why do you want to take the polar bear along?' Noah gave him a look. 'Take along?' 'Yes,' the naturalist continued, 'or shall we say, why do you want the polar bear on your list? A bear can turn white later, all on its own, as long as you have the ordinary brown bear with you, that will suffice. You see, this scroll tells you the bare necessities, everything else can develop from it. Why should Man not make the selection, since there are animals which go extinct all on their own? Think of the dinosaurs—a failed attempt to breed a group of small-skulled races, muscular, thinking with their loins. They died out.' 'But what were they for?' Noah asked curiously. 'As an experiment,' answered the scholar. 'They left their bones behind.'

Noah stared at the scroll with excitement, admiration. 'The animals that survived! What a roll of honour you've made!' 'Nothing honourable about it,' said the scholar sharply. 'It's adaptation. Which is why even today the amphibians still haven't made up their minds. We scholars argue over whether humans are better adapted to be tree-dwellers or steppe bipeds, whether we rely on our arms or our legs to save our skins, whether we're climbers or sprinters. Personally, I incline to include humans as a prehensile species, swinging from branch to branch. It was a superb idea for the apes to develop the thumb, an organ that gave them a firm grasp at last.'

'Rather over-hasty of mankind to give up our fins,' mused Noah. The naturalist picked up his thread. 'They were useless once man had decided to take to dry land.' 'But if the land were to become sea once more,' insisted Noah, hugging the scroll to himself. 'Ah yes,' said the scholar, 'I know your hypothesis. However, as a conscientious scientist, I have to tell you that a long rain such as you imagine is climatologically impossible. I understand you, though, for the end of all things is one of mankind's enduring visions. However, we're not here to talk about that. Well, then, if the earth were to become sea once more, hmph, then man would turn out to have been a kind of dinosaur—a failed attempt to create a race with a mid-sized skull, thinking with their brains, who left only bones behind. Then the fish will begin everything all over again.'

After Noah had said his goodbyes to the naturalist, he locked the door of the room where the scrolls and tomes from the National Institute lay heaped up; he leant against the door and let out a long breath. Then he took a closer look at the naturalist's digest; genus upon genus were listed in different columns, and Noah read how even the most diverse animals with their outré names belonged together in families, how animals that eat one another could be brought together into a peaceful flock; tired and delighted, he murmured, 'Heavenly, it's paradise.'

Noah had noted the names of all the people who had come to see him lately, the names of breeders and herdsmen, dealers in livestock and catchers of birds. He had offended quite a few of them by promising to be in touch once he had his catalogue of creatures, and then, when it arrived, crossing the street to avoid them. He pondered the question of who could help him to get hold of the animals, who could make sure that there were male and female each according to their kind, someone prepared to go out and procure the local fauna as well, and who could take care of the feed. Noah knew that his wife had been hiding away her jewellery and the family silver; she had confessed as much. Now he went down to the cellar, hunted around in the sewing scraps and patchwork pieces until he found a red jingling sack.

As Noah stepped out of the house, he bumped into Erim who stood with his thumbs in his armpits, showing off his clean, scrupulously darned clothing. Before Noah could even say how surprised he was, the camel-drover announced in triumph, 'From the institution,' and then wheedled in Noah's ears, 'Give me some work. I hope the Ark isn't ready yet!' When Noah simply gawped at him, Erim explained, 'I'm cured. I'm like the others now. I'll never stick my hand out under a clear blue sky again, looking for the Flood. I won't make fun of you ever again, I won't stand on the building site and laugh at the workers on the Ark.' He looked around, awestruck and shamefaced. 'I almost couldn't find my way to your house. A fellow can hardly find his way around these days, and I wasn't even away that long, they gave me an early discharge, on probation, they said. Once I was admitted, I had to spend weeks repeating "I'm a good-for-nothing, I'm a good-for-nothing." If I said anything else I would get nothing to eat, and if I didn't say "I'm a good-for-nothing" I wasn't allowed to sleep. How happy I was when at last I was allowed to say "I'm employable, I'm employable." They came and lectured at me, me, who barely went to school. There were three of them taking shifts every day, to teach me that a useful member of society holds down a job. Noah, give me some work.'

Noah drew out the scroll and held it out to him. Since Erim was not a great reader, he drew himself up and squared his shoulders before unrolling it; he furrowed his brow and pursed his lips, then put his face close to the scroll and spelt out, 'Flatworms, bristleworms, roundworms—what am I supposed to do with all these worms, Noah?' 'Help save them,' Noah answered. Erim considered this; when a drop formed at the tip of his nose, he wiped it straight away with great to-do so that Noah could see that Erim had learnt how to use a handkerchief in the institution. Then the camel-drover continued reading, 'Scorpions, grasshoppers, lice—but lice are for crushing.' He looked at Noah, downcast, but Noah moved not a muscle in his face. Then Erim turned back to the scroll, resigned and curious, stumbled over his words and asked, 'What's a gnu?' 'You're reading it wrong,' Noah told him but Erim pointed to the word and asked whether that wasn't a *g*, the first letter? Noah thought about it. 'Wonder where the gnu lives?' Erim shrugged his shoulders, then Noah cut short any such considerations. 'We'll take the gnu along. I'm eager to see what it even looks like.'

'Aren't the animals from hereabouts good enough?' Erim began to dicker. 'Why do you need all these foreign beasts? Why do you want to save animals that don't even exist in these parts? And the wild animals as well. Noah, I'm telling you, you're making it harder on yourself with these wild animals. Take the tame ones, think of this Flood as an opportunity, then once it's all over they won't fight and bite any longer.' Noah looked at him sternly, his tongue behind his lower lip. 'I only meant to say,' said Erim, rubbing his hands, 'not that I'd be afraid, I'm a camel-drover, I'm used to dealing with animals. But no one would think the less of you if you were just to stick to the local animals, the tame ones. This Ark is costing you enough already, after all.' Then Noah showed him the bag that he had kept hidden until that moment. It shone and twinkled. Erim put his hands in front of his eyes but then spread his fingers just a little and stared in amazement through the gap. Noah reached into the bag and Erim put his ear to it; it sounded better than coins, full of promise. 'All real?' asked Erim in delight and Noah told him that it was. 'We'll take this jewellery and bring it to life.'

Noah took a ring from the sack; he held it up to the sun, then tried to fit it onto Erim's ring finger but it was too small. 'My mother-in-law had small hands,' said Noah, and Erim held out his little finger, rubbed the stone on his jacket until Noah explained that this kind of stone never lost its shine, and pulled out a necklace. 'We'll catch crocodiles with this.' Erim stooped so that Noah could hang the chain around his neck. 'My wife wore that necklace when we were married,' Noah said reminiscently and Erim laughed out loud. 'Wait till I tell that to my wife!' Noah reached into the sack again, when he opened his hand, loose gemstones lay in his palm. 'Carnelians.'

'They shine like rabbit's eyes,' said Erim in wonder. 'Do you have pockets?' asked Noah, and Erim made sure that there were no holes in his trouser pockets; two little bulges grew at his hips. 'And what about the bracelet?' asked Erim, all agog. 'That could buy a whole herd . . .' Noah interrupted him, 'No herds, no flocks. Six specimens of every animal, three breeding pairs, then one is bound to survive.' Noah put the bracelet around Erim's wrist and was already holding a coronet in his hand. Erim lowered his head and Noah placed the coronet upon his brow. 'Animals and nothing but,' said Noah and held the bag high. 'Will you help me work my magic, Erim?'

'I won't nod,' said Erim apologetically, 'or I'll lose this coronet.' He pulled in his belly to see how far down the necklace hung. Then he peered at Noah's sack, already drooling at the corners of his mouth and he no longer felt the drop forming at the tip of his nose. He put a second bracelet around his ankle, grabbed rings from the sack, shoved a ring onto each finger, and, since he didn't have enough, he put a second ring onto one. In the end, he took the bag himself and jigged it up and down, he stroked it, held it to his cheek, eyes closed, his face beaming. He put one foot in front of the next, his chains and brooches jingling. Erim snapped his fingers, turned round slowly and let the rings gleam and sparkle; his shadow stretched hugely across the square and bent against the wall. He slapped Noah on the back and shouted, 'I'm employed.'

'Hardly discharged from the institution and he's already at it again,' grumbled the lawyer, the timber merchant and the draughtsman, when they heard that Erim was boasting that he would be fetching animals no one had ever seen from regions where no one had ever been. The three of them decided not to beat about the bush; they went straight to Erim's hut and were disconcerted to see a new curtain hanging at his door. Erim lay on a mound of cushions, in a robe with an embroidered hem. 'So here's the man who claimed we were growing rich on Noah's folly, lounging around like a layabout,' began the lawyer. Erim fanned a fly from his face and said that he would like to know just why Noah should be considered mad. 'Because he's building his ship on sand,' said the timber merchant. 'Because he's building a shop with an on-board dovecote,' added the draughtsman. 'Don't you pretend that you find this all quite reasonable,' blustered the lawyer. Erim took a cushion in his arms. 'Why shouldn't this whole shooting match come to an end some time—wham, bam?' He plucked at the cushion and drew out a feather. 'This poor goose was plucked bare and here I am lying in comfort; let's hope she had fun with the cook.' He threw the feather in the air, watched it drift down in zigzags and puffed. 'And aren't human beings plucked bare as well? Perhaps one day we'll all find ourselves stuffed into an enormous cushion and God-knows-who will be lolling upon it at ease.'

Erim got up and dusted his robe with the fan. 'What may I offer you gentlemen? What do you have against me, exactly? That I waited so long to get started? Without you, I would be living in this hut for a lot longer.' He closed his fan and tapped at a beam and wood dust trickled from a hole; he drew back his right sleeve, and the visitors saw a bracelet on his forearm. Erim approached and the others were astonished to smell soap on him; he nodded with a smile, as though to say that a man must embrace his fate. 'Here, a scroll to show you what's going on. Noah, himself, is taking care of the animals which have been crossed out but I'm in charge of the rest.' A highland Turk came into the hut carrying leather satchels. 'I will be away a great deal,' Erim explained. He let a few coins fall to the floor as a tip and pushed them towards the highland Turk with his foot. 'Yes,' he said, turning to his visitors, 'you read on, you're reading it right. Pests and vermin are to be saved but not ourselves. Is that unreasonable?'

When the first animals arrived, the gilded youth of Mesopotamia were learning a new dance.

For an age now, Ham had been promising left and right, when the fancy took him, to invite people to a party such as Mesopotamia had never seen the like; he offered the Ark as a venue. For years and years he had failed to keep his promise, so that 'an invitation from Ham' came to mean 'a pig in a poke'. Many of the young men who had caroused through the night with him and shared women were now married; others had moved away; almost all had chosen a more sober way of life which forbade them from dwelling too much on their youthful adventures. Ham himself was still baby-faced, his stubble soft, his mouth seeming as though it had never been kissed, only a rare gleam flashing in his eyes; but when he waved his hands as he talked you saw what a cool hand he could play.

Ham made good on his promise once the workers had won their dispute with Noah. Even though they were promised extra pay, they refused to work on the Ark at night by moonshine and torchlight, so the site fell quiet after sunset. A few guards were posted to make sure that not too much wood was filched or too many tools stolen, but they were easily bribed, especially since it was Noah's son handing out the hush money. Ham was pleased to be able to send invitations, at last, for this party. He had to do something about his poor reputation; as he grew older, he lost his knack for seduction, even though his pleas and promises became ever more convincing.

When the date of the party at the Ark began to be whispered around, Ham found himself besieged; people came reminding him of old promises and older friendships, recalling adventures shared and money lent. Ham didn't want to invite them all, especially the underage petitioners who were most eager. He asked them not to talk about it too much in advance, they all knew how sometimes girls felt bad when they got home the next day and blurted out everything that they had got up to. Since he couldn't stem the tide, he drew up the guest list for the evening, the night, by asking each one what wickedness he could boast of, and the postulants outdid one another in flights of fancy.

Since the Ark's steps were dismounted each evening to stop lovebirds from coming aboard to spend the night, Ham's guests had to be drawn up into the ship on ropes; they put the girls into baskets, then left them dangling halfway up and let the baskets drop back down a foot or two, but hauled them up onto the deck in the end. The more daring types clambered up the beams. Up on top, they gathered to admire the view; only a few buildings reached this height, and from here on the Ark you could see the rooftops. They crept into the Ark's interior like smugglers, one behind the other, hand on the shoulder in front, and under the cover of darkness indulged in a sly bit of groping. No one had been inside the Ark before, there was no entry for unauthorized persons. The interior stairway was already finished, even if the railings were missing, and so they felt their way forward into the belly of the Ark.

'And what shall we do now?' They put timbers together as benches, grouped within earshot of one another. They talked about what they ought to be learning and boasted of the excuses they had made up to tell their parents; they teased one another, one lad saying how another had looked after the last party—pale—and everyone laughed. A quiet, young, apprentice potter wanted to sing a folk tune but the rest asked him to save it for later. They joshed one another and stroked the girls who knelt at their feet or leant over their shoulders. The usual scene broke out; a girl had spotted an ex-boyfriend, she shouted in his face that he had a limp dick; her target shot back that she padded her breasts. The girl, who just a moment ago had been swinging her hips, now wiped tears from her face with her hair and whispered, 'But my carpets are good,' for she was a carpet-weaver. 'Crap,' shouted some, while others said, 'That's true, though.' Two young men started a fight about it; the others looked on until their blows started to land below the belt, then someone stepped in and made them shake hands. Meanwhile, some couples had gone looking for privacy; the others, flushed and excited from the fight, talked themselves up a storm and stroked and pawed at one another; if it fell quiet for a moment, they could hear the sighing and groaning. Someone who was new to these parties hooted aloud to test the echo. Two friends glared at him; little by little, they all went their ways only to meet again as they gathered up scattered garments.

One girl, though, came back from her corner holding a bunch of dry grass in her hand. 'Hay,' Ham called. 'That's my clever dad!' The girl held out the hay to all the others, telling them to sniff at it. Everyone wanted to know what this was supposed to be good for. 'One more invention,' said Ham, shaking with laughter, 'he's invented a whole lot more than that.' He asked a few to come along with him, and they helped him roll a barrel out to the front and struck off the lid; chunks of something swam in a dark sauce. Someone stuck his finger inside and then licked it clean. 'Sour!' 'Yes,' said Ham, 'It's meat soused in vinegar. Dad says it lasts longer that way.' A boy chewed at a piece of the meat and declared that it wasn't so sour after all. 'It has spices in it.' Now the others took a taste as well, shoved meat into their mouths, spat it out or savoured it, giggled, threw it at one another, swore and threw it back if the first wouldn't give up, hollered and, in the end, heaved the barrel over so that the souse meat and the sauce ran over the deck of the Ark.

Then the quiet, young, apprentice potter stepped out from the crowd and wanted to sing his folk tune. Ham yanked him aside though, so fiercely that he almost fell over. Ham stood beneath a porthole where moonlight streamed in. 'You can say what you like about the children of Cain but we've them to thank for the pipers and drummers.' Everyone guffawed. 'Yes, I'm musical,' Ham bragged and beat a rhythm on his thigh; he put his head to one side and slowly rolled up his eyes. 'So are we,' whooped the guests. 'D'you want to try a dance?' asked Ham, and talking over the applause as it came, 'They have taught us to honour our fathers, so let's dance to my father's honour.' Ham took off his shirt, the girls craned their necks to see (some of them not for the first time) the much-admired and much-appreciated half-moon tattoo on his biceps and not a few squeezed their partners' muscles appraisingly, comparing.

Ham held out his arms, testing for rain first with the backs of his hand and then with the palms; he looked up at the open hatch overhead. 'Hey, it's drizzling!' Ham looked down at himself quickly but then pointed straight upwards again. 'It's starting to rain. Where's the music?' He gazed about, then asked one of them to take a spar of wood and beat time on the floor; he told another to saw up the barrel but in time with the beat. 'More rain,' he demanded, and the beat became louder. 'I'll show you the steps,' said Ham, beginning the class, and put his left leg forwards. 'One leg gets wet,' he lifted it and shook it, 'the other leg gets wet.' He put the first foot back down and lifted the second, shaking that leg, then hopped, 'a puddle!' The others hopped along in time but Ham silenced them with a gesture. 'The water's rising. We're swimming. Now the dance begins; downpour-hey, downpour-ho!' The chorus thumped along. 'A towel!' called Ham, and the girls moved to take off their headscarves but Ham refused them all, 'I'll dry with air, I'll dry myself with nothing.' He moved as though rubbing his back dry, thrust one thigh forwards and then the other, circling his shoulder blades. 'At "down" you fling your arms out in front, at "pour" you pull them back and at "hey-ho" you fold them close. Don't forget to dry yourself!' Everyone watching took up the first pose.

'No couples,' Ham commanded. 'Everyone dances on their own—in the round!' He urged the wooden spar and the saw to keep up and stamped out the beat with his feet once more. 'No bumping into one another!' Everyone looked for rain and moonlight fell onto their hands through the hatch; they leapt over puddles and hopped over the soused meat where it lay. 'The barrel thunders and the stave beats the rain,' Ham shouted out, 'the raindrops are falling thick and fast, dry yourselves down!' The dancers swayed on the waves. They swam past one another, waved at one another until swept away by a gust of wind; for a little while they formed couples, whirling and swirling, then the rhythm sped them onwards, staggering, they formed threes and braved the waves until a billow flung them apart. The sweat trickled down inside their clothes, they unbuttoned shirts and loosened blouses. Ham lashed them onwards with every 'down', every 'pour', every 'hey' and 'ho', dragging back any dancer who wanted to stop. But too many gave up, standing in a circle at the edge, beating time with their hands, thirsty, tired, exhilarated; they egged on those who were still dancing, driving them through the water. Only the wooden stave never let up; more and more dancers dropped out, more and more stood and looked on at the few who could keep up until there was only one, dancing, frenzied and unflagging.

Then came a roar that made most of them clutch the wooden walls but the wood trembled too. Then it fell quiet; a girl giggled. Another roar. All eyes strained in the darkness to see where the sound came from; hands reached out to hands. A spar clattered against the floor, the silence stretched on, the tension; someone pulled his shirt over his head and joked, 'It's a ghost.' But no one made a sound, they hastened to dress. They heard a scratching, beams being hauled aside and bolts shot back; the sidewall gaped and a lion wriggled through the opening. He bit at the poles shoving him into the Ark, and flung his head about to try to escape from the noose around his neck. In the grey light, the camel-drover and Noah appeared. 'There are people here.' Then the lion roared thunderously. Everyone who had spotted the animal screamed at once and ran for the stairs, shoving their way through, barging past one another, dragging their partner along and then leaving him to fend for himself, trampling anything that lay on the floor. The moon shone through the hatch to show the way and a cry came up from the darkness, 'Save yourselves from the Ark!'

'What's Noah up to now?' the Mesopotamians asked one another, 'What does he call this invention then?'

Though the mothers and fathers were furious about the party in the Ark, they were glad that their sons and daughters had managed to escape from the wild animals, even if one girl had lost her speech and had to go into therapy for the trauma. Soon enough, news got out that Noah was storing up things like hay and soused meat in the Ark. Some remembered that they had seen Noah out mowing grass. The party-goers from the Ark were scolded and beaten at home at first but they were also stopped on the street and asked how hay smells and whether soused meat is edible. The lads and lasses smacked their lips and gave their verdict; they were the first ever to have eaten iron rations.

The wild animals, though, were a threat, even if they were only driven through the streets at night. When a monkey broke loose, everyone was entertained; no one captured him despite the large reward that was announced, and the monkey was fed wherever he turned up. Yet, everyone said, next time it may be something more dangerous. The lawyer advised Noah, as his best client, to be more circumspect and not stir up the public. Noah accepted the advice but refused to do without even one of his animals; he promised to take steps, however. One morning, he called in on the lawyer, accompanied by a black panther. The lawyer fled through the back door while his scrivener piled up a hasty barricade of chairs. The black beast behaved quite peacefully, however. The lawyer peered through the window back into his own room, wondering why the animal wasn't making a sound, and the scrivener raised his head cautiously, almost annoyed that nothing had been clawed or ripped to pieces. Noah waved both of them closer, leant over the animal and pointed at its head; he had taken leather straps and bound them together around the animal's chops, tying the whole contrivance tight at the nape. 'He can breathe but he can't bite.' Noah held out his finger, the panther tried to open its mouth but could hardly even bare his teeth. 'A muzzle,' explained Noah. Then the animal lashed at Noah with its paws, tore at his clothes with its claws, and under the tatters they could see bloody stripes form as the animal fell back on all fours. 'We should invent some kind of gloves for the animals, next,' said Noah abstractedly, dabbing as the blood welled up freely.

'What's this supposed to be?' people asked on another morning when they saw him with a pole over his shoulder with a net at the end. One of them followed and watched from a distance as Noah ran through the field, swatting at the air with his net and pole. 'He's fishing in the air,' reported the eyewitness, and soon people learnt that Noah had invented a butterfly net. Next, Noah daubed a piece of cloth with honey and hung it up. Flies came and stuck fast, creeping to a slow death; Noah had, in fact, wanted to capture the flies for the Ark but their wings were gummed up and when he took the cloth down it was black with dead flies.

They only mocked the flypaper for a little while and then plenty of people began to copy it. They smeared less honey onto the cloth so that it didn't drip, and after that no one had flies in their rooms, and it was generally agreed that a man who sets out to build an Ark can nevertheless have a surprising dose of common sense. The flypaper gave a trader the idea of going to ask Noah whether he had any other inventions that might be worth investing in. Noah's wife was embarrassed and hesitated a long while, not knowing whether she should say anything but in the end she showed him a jar. The trader tasted some and was astonished. 'Berries,' he said, and licked clean a second spoonful, 'but not just berries. Other fruit in there as well.' 'Yes,' said Noah's wife, 'cooked down with honey, stirred well and then sealed with leaves; it keeps well and stays sweet, even if it gets a bit furry on top.' The trader scooped up spoon after spoon, not saying a word, licked the spoon and licked his thumb and then his lips. He hurried outside and was sick up against a wall, then came back, brisk and delighted. He had never been sick before from eating anything so tasty; others would certainly like it too. He used his charms to worm the secret out of her and Noah's wife was glad to get a little money for nothing more than giving away the recipe.

Noah chose a time of day for his hunts when no one was on the streets, which is how he was caught out himself in the early hours. 'What are you doing there?' Noah was surprised to recognize Chlea's voice; he stayed down on his knees but raised his head. 'I'm looking for a mouse.' Next to Noah, stood a pot with a fist-sized hole in the side, upturned on a board. Noah lifted the pot and showed the hunk of bacon inside. Then he propped the pot back on its board and bent down again to the ground. Chlea spotted the mousehole. 'Come along little mouse,' cooed Noah, 'you be a good little mouse. Come along, mousey. Are you coming then? We've got an Ark for you, a great big Ark. Come along, hurry up. Do you hear? Out you come. If you don't come out, I'll fetch the cat. Hurry along now.' Chlea set her finger on Noah's lips, nodded politely to the mouse and spoke silently. Then the mouse stuck its nose out, sniffed, whiskers atremble; it slipped out of the hole, scampered about indecisively, climbed onto the piece of wood and then vanished into the pot. Noah put his hand over the opening at once. 'The mouse is in there, there's the mouse. Without that bacon, the mouse would never have made it onto the Ark.'

'You're up early,' said Noah, stretching in the morning sunlight. Chlea fished her necklace up from her bosom and ran the pearls between her lips, saying, 'I've seen you often enough. You're not just up early, you're out all night as well.' 'I need less sleep as I get older,' Noah said, nodding. 'Oh, it's not that though, is it?' said Chlea, wagging a finger at him. 'I've followed you often enough too.' Noah put his head on Chlea's shoulder. 'Jasmine?' he asked. 'Mixed with roses,' Chlea agreed, 'Does it smell too strong? It shouldn't, you know. Otherwise they go home smelling of me,' and Chlea sniffed at herself but then picked up the conversation once more, 'From one trench to the next.' Noah laughed—his guilty secret discovered—cheerfully and confessed, saying that he liked to see how the earth was sliced open, how the clays and gravels were layered, excavation fascinated him, he could look at the strata without a care in the world, then he stopped for a moment and added, apologetically, that what he really liked about buildings was the foundation—something you really had to understand, if you were to build something the size of the Ark with no foundation at all.

Once they were walking alongside one another, Chlea linked arms. The first timber carriers were already at work; a couple let the beam slip from their shoulders when they saw the two of them walking. The first shouted commands were heard across the site, while hammer blows startled birds into flight from the scaffolding. Chlea hummed a tune and tapped time with her fingers on Noah's arm while he hugged the mousetrap close. Suddenly, Chlea tightened her grip. 'I'm stubborn too but sometimes I forget myself. You never lose sight.' She amused herself by matching her stride to Noah's long steps; he felt comfortably happy. When Chlea wanted to stop still, he tugged her arm and took her onwards. 'You dodge the blows,' said Chlea, swinging her handbag. 'Nothing that goes on around you makes any difference to you.' Noah raised his brows, 'Do you think so? What do people say who haven't been following me from one trench to the next at night?' His words broke up into laughter. 'The mouse is tickling me. It's fed up with running about in circles.' 'Invent something for me,' Chloe challenged him. She let go of his arm and sketched in the air the shape of the invention she wanted. 'Something that brings them in like flypaper but doesn't keep them stuck. Something as secure as a mousetrap but that you can leave when you want. Something that stays good like jam and smells like hay. Something to make this life bearable.'

'Something's going to happen,' the Mesopotamians prophesied. 'But what?'

When Noah had gone to the doctor, many people were secretly sympathetic; money can't buy you happiness, they thought. When the animals began to arrive, though; and when Erim explained how he earned his money; when there was talk of new consignments; when Noah's house went to wrack and ruin so that the passers-by talked about how he had stopped caring for his home and spent his whole time on the Ark; when word got out that Noah was selling his wife's jewellery, no one was surprised by Shem's behaviour.

'Talk sense,' Shem said, blocking his father's path. 'This time I won't be fobbed off with excuses. So far I've just gritted my teeth and put up with it.' 'What are you after?' asked Noah. 'My right as firstborn but I know that you can't give it—you squandered it long ago,' Shem accused. 'Not at all,' said Noah, 'you'll get one third of the animals, I'm taking one breeding pair for each of my sons. If animals die en route, I'll take them out of Ham's tally, you can be sure of that.' 'It's easier for you to save all Creation than to care for your own family,' said Shem mockingly. 'I'm doing it for you as well,' Noah replied. 'I know the sentimental tale,' Shem laughed. 'You heard it from your mother. Of course there were tears in my eyes the first time I saw you—tears of rage. One more, and my fault, but now I need you.' 'No one else works as cheap,' said Shem bitterly. Noah tried to explain that he had the strength to go on but didn't know why; he had no reason to go on, his sons must give him reasons, maybe it was unfair on his part, he said, that he hadn't brought up sons, just reasons. 'We've even had to take our children out of school,' complained Shem. 'They'll have time to help in the stables,' mused Noah. Shem shut his eyes, furious. Then Noah grabbed hold of a stick and let fly at his eldest son. 'I'll drive you aboard the Ark!'

This time Shem sought no one's advice and didn't even consult his wife. He hesitated a while about whether he should wait until the blows had faded from his face and hands but then he decided to go to court with these proofs so that his scars and bruises would argue just as eloquently as his words. The blood crusting his face would be his best witness when he came to Yegerom. On the way, he met the lawyer who straight away spread word of what Shem was probably after.

When the news came that Shem had been spotted, everyone ran, wanting to hear at firsthand whether he had been able to have Noah declared non compos. The draughtsman and the timber merchant ran too, more nervous than the rest, angered at everyone else's unseemly curiosity. The timber merchant said fretfully, 'Shem is dangerous.' 'He looks it,' said the draughtsman, pointing at Shem who stood by a wall, his robe torn at the shoulder, his face smeared with dust and sweat, a wound on his brow. Everyone wondered whether he had been attacked on the way to Yegerom or whether this was how the court had treated him.

'Water,' whispered Shem. Noah, who had just joined the crowd, asked mockingly, 'Isn't there enough water in Yegerom?' Shem groaned without looking up. His wife brought a bucket but Shem drank the water that she had thought to use for washing his wounds. When he tried to wipe his mouth he could no longer lift his arm. His mother tore a piece of cloth into strips but Shem waved away her attempts to help and blurted out his son's name. He hadn't noticed that the child was clinging to his robe; he pulled the boy in front of him, grasping his shoulder with his good hand so that the little lad cried out for his mother, but his father kept a grip on him, using him to stay upright. 'It rained from below,' Shem whispered. Then Noah looked up at the clear blue sky.

'Yegerom has drowned,' Shem began. His audience shouted with horror, clamoured with questions, called out the name of relatives, asked for more information and details. 'I didn't understand,' Shem reported, 'why so many people were crowding into the court when I took the stand.' Spittle and blood filled Shem's mouth, but when he tried to spit his chest squeezed tight. 'I woke up on a hill and felt my wounds, which is how I knew I was saved.' 'Leave him alone,' shouted Noah's wife, fighting her way through the crowd towards him, but she was held back. 'They rushed up from the cellar, the prisoners and guards. The guards let the prisoners free from their chains and gave them buckets to bail out but there weren't enough buckets. The judge called for order and then threw away his bell. Everyone fled, in their wigs and gowns or their prisoners' overalls, but there was only one upper floor and nothing above that. The dam broke, the sea came. It got the marketplace first, claimed the fish and the fishwives, and then the sea reached the courthouse, came in through the portal but not just one step at a time. The files left the courthouse. The law books sank straight away, the writs and the sentences floating off. Pardons blowing in the wind. A witness stand and a judge's chair floating along behind.'

'At last,' said Chlea, clapping her hands. Shem had collapsed, his mother and wife were holding him and offering comfort that he could no longer refuse. Noah looked down at the ground by his feet. 'Why are you distraught?' Chlea called out to them. 'This whole time you've been hoping for the Flood, hardly do you get a taste of it than the eyes pop out of your heads. You'll need these eyes, though. How else are you going to climb a mountain?' She took Erim's hand and held it. 'Even Erim wears his faith on his sleeve! Please don't cry or the water will rise even higher. Yes, knocking shop's closed. I'll blow the signal to halt.' She held her cupped hands before her mouth and trumpeted. Then she opened her bag and took out a compact, scattering powder into the air, saying, 'The wind should be as pale as you all are.' She shut one eye as though to test the wind's pallor, dabbed at it once more with her brush and then squirted some scent. 'I'll pretty it up,' Chlea said gleefully, 'I'll powder the wind's nose. It must look its best if it's bringing us the clouds.' The square smelt of jasmine mixed with roses.

It proved impossible to establish whether anyone had in fact shoved Chlea; no one saw anyone trip her, and she must have fallen on her own. Nor was it clear whether anyone had thrown a stone, though it seemed unlikely; the stones where she lay were already there when she fell, and if she had been trampled, it was only because everyone was pushing to see, with those behind crushing those in front. The wound at her temple was caused by the fall. When the doctor bent over her, holding a mirror to her mouth and feeling her pulse, she was already dead and someone said, 'She's still showing her legs even in death.'

Everyone assured one another that they would not attend Chlea's funeral but nearly everyone came nevertheless, just to see, and was duly surprised at how many had come just to see. As decency demanded, the women stood back, the wives keeping a close eye on their husbands but the husbands showing nothing on their stony faces. The priest walked next to the bier which was draped with a costly cloth; many present wondered who had paid for it. The priest said straight off that he did not want to speak at length; he spoke only of Chlea's childhood and youth, of how even as a little girl she had helped her mother do the shopping and looked after her brothers and sisters. Everyone listening considered for the first time the fact that Chlea had been a girl once, but they all waited with bated breath to hear what the priest would say about the years when they had known Chlea. But the priest merely said that she had not had an easy life, which made the women glare furiously. Since the priest did not want to talk of what she had done in life, he talked about her hair, how it had been so fine that no comb could tame it, so that she wore headbands which many had then imitated. While he praised her headwear in his eulogy, he also traced her figure in the air with his hand.

When the priest took up the shovel, Noah leapt forwards, tore it from his hand and didn't even try to lift a spadeful but simply shoved soil into the grave with the blade and with his feet. 'Let's have one more burial here on dry ground.' A second man came forwards from the throng without looking backwards at the women. Noah handed him the shovel without giving up his place; he grabbed handfuls from the heaps of earth. Others filed forwards, shared the work, lending a hand, and, where they were too heavy, joined forces to throw the clods down onto Chlea. The timber merchant and the draughtsman held onto one another's shoulders and shoved earth into the grave with the sides of their feet. Erim tumbled and almost fell into the grave, slipping deep enough to get a shovel full of earth in his face; when he climbed out, his eyes were watering. When the hole had been filled in and the mound that had been heaped up next to Chlea's grave now lay atop her, they stamped it flat with hands and the shovel, pushing one another aside and crowding together, Noah amid them saying over and over, 'Lucky to have died when she did, when there was still enough earth to put her underground.'

The Mesopotamians took the Flood that had destroyed Yegerom as a chance to show their charity and pause for reflection.

The victims of the Flood had to be helped; despite the general devastation, a few had survived. The timber merchants supplied wood at cost price, while the ornamental woodcarvers set their apprentices to work, in regular hours rather than overtime, to carve little anchors as badges—delicate objects in two different designs, the more expensive with two ribbons wreathed about it to represent the two rivers. The children were given three afternoons off school to take to the streets and squares to sell the little anchor badges. Part of the money was to go to build a monument showing the exact date of the catastrophe and the estimated number of victims. This initiative won general praise for being so straightforward and was accompanied by a minute's silence; for sixty seconds, tools were downed all across Mesopotamia, conversation cut short, all work and any kind of noise stopped while they thought of their fellow men on the river.

The event of the season, though, was the charity banquet hosted by the timber merchant; the upper classes decided that they were most obliged, that they must do more than the others and do it in their own particular way. The timber merchant would dearly have loved to have Noah as guest of honour. When Noah refused, the timber merchant thought at first that he was ashamed to be seen in his usual scruffy clothes and offered to lend him a robe for the occasion. Noah didn't take him up on the offer, though.

Ham, who had just come into the room, offered to act as master of ceremonies; he suggested water sports out in the garden.

The timber merchant, though, didn't give up; he came to see Noah again, not alone this time but bringing the chef with him. The chef bowed so low that his toque almost fell from his head; he shoved it back into place, slightly crooked as tradition demanded, rather flustered. 'How should I begin?' He rumpled his nose as though he could already smell all the odours, lifted his hands high as though lifting the lid from a pot. 'I'm not much with words, Noah. I cater to the palate, not to the ears.' 'I don't know about that,' the timber merchant interrupted, 'you've always got a lot to say in the kitchen.' 'I'll start the same way we start a meal then, with the first course,' the chef began again, clasping his hands behind his back and sticking out his belly as though it were a table to deck; he talked with his eyes to the ground. 'Should I recommend the turbot or the bream, given that I've lavished as much love on either? I was at the marketplace myself. The trout are not lake trout but straight from the stream.' Noah sucked at a straw so that the chef said coquettishly, 'Noah doesn't seem terribly fond of fish.' 'I'm not mad about fish myself,' said the timber merchant, finishing with the first course, 'because of the bones and the way their little eyes stare up so sadly from the dish.'

'I don't just serve fish,' the chef shot back, slighted, 'not just crab and mussels.' He tied his apron more tightly. 'Do you like a bird? I have roasted nightingales that come back to life on your tongue to sing. There'll be no shortage of poultry.' 'Don't forget the turkey,' the timber merchant put in. 'Oh indeed, indeed,' said the chef, his eyes twinkling, his jowls grinning, 'turkey with truffles. Truffles, now there's a marvellous tuber. Makes women more willing, you know. As a chef, I always have to consider what the guests might get up to after the meal, ho ho! I know my onions.' Noah spat out the straw and turned away. 'Not hungry.' The chef clapped his hands in bewilderment and stammered, 'I can spice it as you like it. Name your dish. Whatever Nature created, I roast it and cook it, you can have it steamed or sautéd, rare or well done.' The chef pulled the ladle from his apron string and waved it in the air. 'Stuffed hare . . . we've laid in shoulder of venison, leg of mutton, ox tongue and escalope of veal. Noah, please, Noah, just a little bit of one of these delicacies, a forkful. At least come to see for yourself. I can't persuade you but the sight of the food will make you want to eat.' The chef smacked his lips. 'Delicious.' But Noah was already gone. The chef snorted, drew himself up and yelled after him, 'What an oik!' The timber merchant, impatient and upset, gave the chef a piece of his mind. 'One doesn't say, "Not hungry", one says "I have other commitments,"' the chef grumbled and then suddenly grabbed at his toque. 'My signature dish! I forgot to mention the roast doves with their olive branch in the beak!'

At the charity dinner, the first serious complaints about Noah were spoken aloud; not that they were spoken directly as such. When two donors met at the long buffet table where the dishes were set out, one said to the other, as they chose between the chicken breast and the crab, 'If it weren't for Noah, we'd have just seen this Flood as what it is—the kind of natural disaster that can happen anywhere.' And the other waved a hand. 'Can't even talk about the weather these days.' While the men eyed the women's cleavage approvingly and the women sized up one another's dresses, someone said quite suddenly and with no preamble, 'Be all that as it may, I didn't care for how Noah behaved at Chlea's funeral. Who knows what their actual relationship was.' 'Oh, God!' and the conversation was over. And when two diners sat down together, their empty plates perched on their knees, resting after the feed, then one would say with his well-fed mouth to the well-fed face next to him, 'Well, that was better than a plate of hay, wasn't it?' A poet was also invited to the charity dinner to read a new work—in free verse, as he explained, and with nothing resembling a rhyme—a poem about the two armies which marched on Yegerom, one army on four legs and one on two, an army of soldiers and an army of rats, both on clean-up duty.

People in Mesopotamia told one another that panic is one thing but taking necessary precautions is quite another, and they began to make plans.

The business community had been looking forward with apprehension to the day that the Ark was finished, though not quite in despair, but they only began to discuss the matter when the interior was being fitted out. When two businessmen met, they would leap straight past the routine questions about health and family and instead speak with all their commercial wits about them, to the point, their phrasing sharpened by giving dictation, quite used to directness. 'Is the crisis coming? It can't carry on as it has done these last few decades, that would be ridiculous, we don't live in a school textbook. Noah alone is a poor basis on which to develop your economy. Not that we would find ourselves strapped, of course, but we certainly have to prepare for some setbacks, it's only reasonable. Time's come to see who can stay the course and who fixed the roof while the sun was shining.'

The bankers and money-changers were still giving short-term loans and demanding collateral, and they made a joint statement to the press and public, saying that it was the wrong moment for panic. The statement was particularly directed at the small depositors who for unclear and reprehensible reasons of their own were queuing up to withdraw their savings. An accountant absconded, causing further consternation, although the bank affected issued repeated assurances that the disappearance was no cause for panic. General prosperity, they said, was built on mutual trust; the fact that fewer loans were being approved didn't mean by a long chalk that there was no credit to be had; the main thing was to maintain confidence for the future, even if the stock market was no longer so lightly regulated. This was not a slump, they declared, merely a regression to the norm, even perhaps a salutary shock to the system. The fact that everyone had it good did not mean that everyone would always have it better.

A government spokesman also made a statement. 'The voters know that I'm going in to bat for

the miracle that underpins our economy.' He came
from a working-class family and liked to present
himself as a man of the people; he had bought the
hut where he had been born, saved it from demoli-
tion and had it restored to its original condition.
'Don't be fooled, though,' he warned. He suffered
from high blood pressure and sweated when he got
worked up; when he gave a speech, he always had a
handkerchief to hand with which he flagged his
important sentences or waved in greeting to his listeners and dismissed hecklers and he also used it to
mop his brow and his neck. 'Honest work isn't wage
slavery and it's not exploitation. We've worked to put
the living wage in place, so now let's get to work on
a living society. No one in this country has to go
hungry or thirsty, no one has to pay strangers for the
privilege of having a roof over his head. We're a
country where the sun shines and everyone has their
own little shady nook, and even in the humblest hut
the drinks are kept cool. Don't be fooled. Let's enjoy
ourselves within limits and then we'll never experience unlimited misery. Enjoy what you've earned
but you'll never enjoy anything if you don't work
for it. I'm bold enough to believe in prosperity for
all but that means I'm bold enough give unpopular
warnings as well. Be reasonable and remember that

reason begins at home. If you're not prepared to look facts in the face, you're cutting off your own nose to spite your face. Look where we've ended up. These days everyone can afford fresh rolls for a bank-holiday breakfast but we end up eating yesterday's rolls. Why? Because the bakers refuse to bake on a bank holiday.'

A few days after the government spokesman gave his warning, and after the bankers and money-changers had issued their statement, respected businessmen nevertheless announced that they were insolvent. The word 'insolvent' sounded new and no one was quite sure what it meant. Some of these insolvent businessmen were still seen in fashionable bars and restaurants but others were said to have gone abroad, others again sought peace and quiet for health reasons, and one was quite definitely known to have killed himself. The surprise was that these were businessmen whose warehouses covered whole city blocks, and the man on the street believed that nothing could happen to fat cats like that since, after all, they had the goods. But this was exactly the mistake. The man who had cornered the market in tar had stored the supply to sell it at the opportune moment. The Ark, though, was already tarred, and he was left with the goods on his hands.

Greater disquiet only broke out once workers were laid off from the Ark, not all at once even; some were kept on for the stalls, pens, stables and other fittings and interiors. Once the Ark stood there, gleaming, smelling of fresh wood and of pitch, its viewports to all four quarters of the compass planed smooth; once the tween decks had not just been swept of sawdust but washed down; once the off-cuts and shavings had been burnt for days on end; once all the ramps were tested and the doorframes checked to see that the doors sat snug; once the stakes had been hammered home which held the Ark steady in the wind—then the labourers all stood in amazement in front of their handiwork with a feeling of pride. Many paced out the length of the Ark and many saw the other end of the Ark and its stern, for the first time. They were looking forward to the topping-out ceremony but Noah did not organize one. One of the very old workers fell to reminiscing; now it would be like before, when the workers marched through the streets eight abreast, not just those who had been laid off but also those who still had a job to lose. They didn't say a word but held banners to show what was on their minds. 'What now?' they asked, 'The highland Turks have work,' and 'We will take our children to church

to be fed.' The workers' leaders negotiated with
Noah, and one reminded him that as a young trade
unionist he had fought Noah's corner in a meeting
with the priests and scholars. But Noah revealed that
he had no ready money left and couldn't raise credit;
straight away they asked how he intended to pay the
workers he had kept on for the interior. They agreed
that Noah would mortgage his house and its estate
—everyone knew that it was good land, well-placed
for transport. When the workers' leaders asked
how things were with the meadows and pastures,
Noah admitted that these were already pledged and
re-mortgaged because of the animals. The negotia-
tors made do with what they had got. Nevertheless,
there were banners held up at the hours-long march,
reading, 'Ark yes, Noah no.'

After the first upsets, though, it proved that things
were not as bad as the scaremongers and naysayers
would have it or as the pundits and demonstrators
claimed. First of all, the highland Turks were sent back
where they had come from, so that not just jobs but
homes were freed up. It turned out that, beside the
Ark, there were plenty of building projects underway;
the school-building programme had to scale down
some of its plans but, here too, fears were shown to
have been unfounded. It was a matter of cuts rather

than freezes, and this held true for the road-building programme as well. And then, certainly, people would have to retrain. Many who had so far worked in the building sector, looked for jobs with the livestock traders and breeders, with the livestock dealers and the feed merchants. Millers suddenly came to prominence, especially those who made feed as well as flour. Everyone could see that growth may have slowed somewhat but prosperity remained unaffected. Proof of this was Erim, the camel-drover, and his wife. The whole time that the Ark was being built they had gone around in rags; now, they wore tailored clothes.

Erim's wife sat in the latest chic cafe in the afternoons with other wives, eating cakes and sweetmeats. 'It's dreadful,' and they all nodded, 'with these animals.' Once she had licked her fingers clean, she carried on explaining how terribly busy her husband was. The neighbours only saw the money coming in, she complained, and didn't see how it had to be earned. 'Thank heavens one of the bitches was in oestrus, otherwise the dogs . . .' The other wives looked at her questioningly. 'Oh yes,' Erim's wife said, 'that's the technical term for "in heat". The things my husband has to learn! Noah himself doesn't know all there is to know about animals, you know. Do you know what a male goose is called? A gander. Well, who would have guessed it. And if only my husband even knew for sure that animals are male or female! Look for yourself, next time you catch a millipede, and as for the earth-worm, well, he's still not sure. Not that it makes much of a difference in the end.' She slapped her hand on the table, straight into the pastries, and ordered another plate. It really was something with these animals, she told them, quite ghastly, her hus-band was giving up years of his life; the beavers almost sent him into a nervous collapse, they started gnawing at the Ark as soon as they were aboard.

But despite all kind thoughts and considerate words, Yegerom, Mesopotamia's largest port, had been destroyed. It was a blessing that the army had been deployed to stop the danger of plague, people told one another, and they lined the streets to watch the troops march away to carry out the salvage. For weeks, the ruins of Yegerom were a popular tourist destination with careful checks on visitor numbers. All those who went to see the lake of mud and the ruined city were still thoughtful and downcast as they then stopped in at the souvenir and snack stalls lining the exclusion zone. Everyone agreed that caution was called for, meaning not just that the dams and flood barriers should be built more robustly but in a wider sense. The more prudent founded a company where every interested party could pay a monthly premium, in return for which, its mission statement promised, the company would contractually pay out a fixed amount agreed in advance for any future damage or injury. They called this an insurance company. There's something to this idea of the Flood, they reckoned. But who says that the Flood has to be water? A meteor may fall from heaven, fields may catch fire and houses be burnt to the ground; or the water's poisoned and the death count rises with each meal; or there's an earthquake and the high-rises collapse. The Flood might come stooped and hobbling, called 'old age', or come as an empty spot, a strongbox broken open where you'd been saving your money, and then the Flood was a thief. The deluge might come at any time of the day and at any time of life, barefaced or masked, during your sleep or with all eyes upon it, overpowering or insidious; a broken spine and decades bedridden, a bridge collapsing, a horse kicking over the traces—not to mention all those who fell from scaffolding and broke their necks in the trenches! Of course insurance could not bring a dead man back to life but it could make a new start easier for those who were left behind with tact and care. Of course, an insurance policy couldn't give a blind man back his sight but it could pay for him to have a dog. Insurance never made anyone any younger but it could make life easier for the children and grandchildren. Thus people insured themselves not just against flood but also against fire and theft, hail and plague, accidents and old age. Since the insurance companies, in their turn, were dealing with unpredictable factors, they got together to found a new reinsurance company.

Voices were also raised, however, which said that even these precautions were not enough and they demanded that the schools introduce swimming lessons. Opposing arguments chipped in straight away; well-to-do fathers protested at the idea that the state might force their children to learn to swim at school. The Left, though, argued that everyone had a right to learn to swim, that the basic strokes were the same for everyone, regardless of background or tax bracket, and that a life-or-death matter such as swimming was certainly part of a state-school curriculum. A committee was appointed and, after many sessions and much haggling, submitted its report that swimming should be classed alongside singing and religious studies and introduced as an optional subject.

The gym teachers objected that the committee had included a member of the priesthood but no specialist sports teacher; swimming, they said, was water-borne athletics, not just splashing about. Committee protocols showed that none of the members or expert witnesses had given a thought to the idea that the backstroke and the breaststroke are not the be-all and end-all, that there's the crawl to consider. A swimmer, they said, is someone to take as your model; he has a muscular but not muscle-bound physique, thanks to his well-balanced adipose tissues, and only the swimmer shows that characteristic classical ribcage. The gym teachers relented, though, once they learnt that there were to be three lessons a week and that courses for adults were also planned. The trade unions duly added swimming to their day release and evening classes. The sports teachers promised that they could make young and old into happy water rats.

The Mesopotamians began on dry land, with press-ups and squat thrusts; they learnt the difference between flutter kick and frog kick. Once the learners made their way into the water, the sports teachers took great care with the nervous ones and let the uncertain swimmers know that they could use a float; they also taught the more confident ones how to dive. The teachers had been told to use a favourite method in school, teaching through play so that the pupils learnt without even noticing, almost in their sleep, until they'd got it. So the Mesopotamians played hide-and-seek in the water and piggy-in-the-middle and blindman's bluff.

The craze for swimming gripped all Mesopotamia; they held swimming races and they also erected big towers along the banks of each of the two rivers for exhibition diving. Anyone who was putting on weight or breaking into an unaccustomed sweat or who found that even a few steps left him short of breath was given doctor's orders to swim regularly; this would relax him and help get rid of some tension, it was high time to give some thought to your state of health in an affluent society.

Fashion designers let their imaginations run wild, offering clothes that used a little bit of fabric but a lot of fun; Mesopotamian ladies liked most of all to cover themselves (or not) with very fine-meshed net. There were public debates and family arguments about the navel, with the faction winning out in the end that found nothing wrong with showing one's navel (and looking at other people's). Little huts were built in countless places all along both rivers where people could change into their swimming things. Plenty of those who had previously worked on the Ark now took jobs as bathing attendants, making sure that no one threw their rubbish on the beach or went through clothes lying waiting for their wearers to return. Doctors, soon enough, began to warn that it was by no means healthy to spend hours lying unprotected in the sun; the Mesopotamians had begun to sunbathe, as well as bathe in the water.

The more public-spirited souls were offered courses in lifesaving, much visited by primary-school teachers. Swimmers who were known to be good divers played the role of the drowners, screaming, waving their hands and sinking with loud gurgles. All the options were rehearsed; a drowner might grab the lifesaver's wrist or ankle, might cling to his chest or his throat. It was generally known that drowning swimmers actually hinder rather than help anyone trying to save their lives, just as if they no longer wished to make it to land but simply wanted not to sink alone. Thus the lifesavers were, first of all, taught the grips to get free; they grabbed the drowners ruthlessly by the forehead or by the nose, got them in a merciless hold under the armpits, could roll them briskly over backwards and, in an emergency, knew how to push the drowner off themselves. Since they were training for every eventuality, they also practiced swimming fully clothed.

Once, as Noah was watering his animals, he saw a group on the bank. Those at the back held down the shoulders of those in front and then pushed their heads to one side. When Noah approached, they parted to let him through, then closed the gap behind him as he came. Without quite knowing how, Noah found that he was in the middle of a circle; he called for his animals but the sports teacher took him into his hairy arms and asked him, with a strong grip, to stay where he was. Noah knelt down and then the teacher said, 'Hup,' moved his hand and Noah was rolled onto his back. The teacher bent over him, flipped him onto his stomach, grabbed below the ribcage; he grunted, lifted him like a deadweight and shook his body, 'so that the water flows out of the mouth.' He let him flop back down and stuck his fingers into Noah's mouth. 'Get the sand and the mud out straight away, and anything else that doesn't belong there. No time to lose in getting the airways open.' When Noah looked up, the instructor asked him not to break role.

The teacher showed how you could restore the dead to life. He wrapped a handkerchief around his fingers and pulled on Noah's tongue at regular intervals. 'Under some circumstances you can spend hours pulling at the tongue like this. There are several techniques.' He stood up, put one foot on Noah's back and commented over his shoulder, 'You fold a towel and place it below the victim's back so that their head and neck are tilted back. Kneel down at their side, then wrap your fingers around their ribcage and press on it by leaning in. This is an old trick, though. I'll show you something new now.' He knelt next to Noah, put one hand on the crown of his head and the other beneath his chin, and pushed Noah's head far back, then he drew a deep breath and blew into Noah's nose, gently and evenly, his own mouth open wide while he held Noah's mouth closed with his thumbs. He looked to see whether the ribcage was rising and falling and listened for breath. Everyone took turns to kneel next to Noah and give him the kiss of life, while one was given the job of wiping Noah's mouth and nose between each learner.

'Things have changed in Mesopotamia,' people said but they also wondered whether the change couldn't have happened some other way.

Never before had so many Mesopotamians gone travelling—on holiday, at weekends, bank-holiday breaks, on business or for their health. People who lived by the beach went into raptures about hiking in the hills, in parts so remote from any human habitation that they had to take along their own food; if they met a farmer on their walk, he would put down his scythe for a chat, ask where the holidaymakers had come from and then want to know which beach they recommended for bathing. The Mesopotamians didn't travel on their own, nor indeed as families; they joined up in large groups. They spent jolly holidays in company, eating in great halls and sleeping in dormitories, each coming to bed when they chose but all woken together at the same time. They travelled to see something new. Everyone had already been to the Ark, more than once, and Yegerom wasn't worth visiting twice. They wanted to see people dressed up in quaint folk costume and strange local styles of house-building, to eat exotic dishes and live a little differently for a while. Despite all this, the more they travelled the less they were impressed, though they were ready to pay admission for something really unaccustomed and to explore the back roads and byways. Everywhere was being built and rebuilt. The wells looked more and more like one another and the travellers found the same blocky buildings everywhere they went, with windows placed just like at home, the terraces no bigger and the walls painted the same old colours. Folk from the Tigris liked fresh peppermint with a meat dish, and found that they could order this in the Euphrates region as well. When Erim took his wife on holiday for the first time so that they too could see a bit of the world, the foreign resort served them up Euphrates frumenty as a speciality, just like they had it at home. 'No point going travelling, is there,' Erim's wife declared. 'Six on the Tigris makes half a dozen from Euphrates.'

Certainly much had changed but many felt short-changed. Hardly had they moved into their houses than the facades began to crumble. The wood warped since it hadn't been properly seasoned; the roof tiles weren't laid according to specification; jerry-built chimneys had been poorly planned so that the heat from the fire went straight up and out, or the smoke hung choking in the kitchen. Plaster flaked off the newest houses as though something were infecting the walls. The tenants complained and the landlords brought suits against the architects; these, in turn, sued the builders who served papers on their suppliers. Every building project gener-ally went hand in hand with a court case—a suit for running over budget, over shoddy work or missed delivery dates. And everywhere the same question was put, and put sharply: Wasn't it all built in a hurry, and too cheaply, even though the bills were so high?

Now the complaint heard everywhere was that quality had dropped. Everyone agreed, though, that progress was to blame and there wasn't much you could do about progress. There had been a shortage of labour pretty nearly everywhere. The highland Turks were even working in Mesopotamia's dairies. A gourmet could tell with just the naked eye that the quality of the cheese had gone down drastically. On the other hand, restaurateurs and landlords found that only a very few customers could tell the difference between real herb cheese and some ersatz product, at least once they started charging the same price for both; and they asked themselves why they should go to the extra trouble if no one appreciated it. Now there was a general shortage of skilled hands. Apprentices left their indentureships before they had served out their terms. They had learnt a few tricks of their trades and now counted themselves as fully accredited specialists; they saw no reason to learn any more of these little knacks, if they could make a living with the ones that they had mastered. The master craftsmen pleaded with their foremen not to use the rough edge of their tongue too much, since the clients were all in a hurry and never asked 'What?' but only 'When? When?'

The old people had hoped that, with all this progress, the young folk would have a different sort of life, a better life; but many fathers ended up wondering whether it hadn't just turned out different. Parents learnt that when their sons and daughters went out on an evening then it wasn't to sing Mesopotamian folk songs, even if they did take their instruments with them. Nor was it true that bad behaviour only broke out when Ham was there to egg it on, and the explanation that there were bad influences around no longer held water. It seemed not to be a problem with the company they kept but with the young people themselves. When their sons went off to the country on the weekend then it wasn't to get some fresh air and enjoy the beauties of Nature but to break into empty houses and run riot. They caroused, smashed furniture and broke windowpanes. They tore up flowers in the gardens and trampled all over the beds. For a long time suspicion fell on the highland Turks, thought to be the only ones capable of such senseless acts. But then it came out that the Chief Constable's son and the lawyer's son had started a gang with their own rites of blood brotherhood; they had attacked a woman as she walked home and snatched her bag but then just scattered the money in a ditch and the bag itself was found lying in a field. The parents were nonplussed and went to one another for advice. 'When we went out and stole when we were young, at least we had a reason for it. But since work began on the Ark everyone has earned enough money. Why do they do it when they don't need to?' But the more wages went up, the higher the crime figures climbed.

'It's just different now,' the young people said when their parents questioned them. 'We told them what we thought they needed to know as soon as they were ready to learn,' worried the parents, looking back on their child-rearing efforts. 'We tested them before we sent them off to school or into apprenticeship. They had a thorough check-up twice a year. True enough that good teeth alone don't make you happy but there's never been a generation with such good teeth. We let our daughters learn a career, which would have been unthinkable earlier. Our children never had to do a hand's turn of work at home either. We never asked what they spent their pocket money on. We never asked where they spent their evenings and we let them stay overnight before they'd got engaged.' But the young people hawked up a curt answer and spat it out at them. 'You gave us our freedom so that you could enjoy your own free time.' 'Let's just chill,' the young people said. They would chill out with their father in the morning, clapping him on the shoulder as he sat sour-faced over breakfast, asking, 'Wasn't Mum up for it last night?' And they would chill out with total strangers on the street, punching them in the face and then demanding a handkerchief to wipe the blood from their knuckles. They were too chilled out to button their shirts, though not quite so chilled that they couldn't answer back. Haircuts were not at all chill and were duly avoided but it was chill to say, 'Kiss my arse, I'm not doing it.' The policeman who had spent years studying case files and interrogation records, in order to learn how best to break and enter, counted as totally chilled out. For a long time he was the suspect wanted for questioning; he had worked on cases where he was the guilty party and had often raised the alarm himself after a successful break-in; he was a skilled cat burglar and an auda-cious armed robber. One day he wrote to the Chief Constable, complaining of the incompetence shown in the investigation, confessed everything, giving exact figures and dates and then vanished and was never caught. 'He was chill to the fill,' said the young people admiringly, and couldn't understand why the parents double-locked the doors. 'What's all the fuss about property, everything's insured, isn't it?'

They had worked for years to make sure that everyone had his daily bread, which mostly meant daily work. By daily bread they didn't just mean wheat from the harvest or dough set out overnight to rise, but a roof over everyone's head; they meant shirts enough for a daily change; not just a loaf in the oven but a bed for everyone so that parents and children did not have to sleep together; and they meant soap and time off work. They got to know the better things in life, sliced bread and rolls, black bread and white, fine-ground and wholemeal. But once they had their daily bread they then wanted some butter on it.

With butter they meant not just churned cream but fresh meat, in quantities that would have fed a whole family earlier; shorter hours and higher over-time pay. By butter they meant not just emulsified dairy fats, sweet to the taste when fresh, but colour-ful cloths to put round their necks; not just butter rolled into little pats but carpets on the floor, car-pets even on the wall and a second home; not just butter that could be salted to stay fresh but savings, interest, premiums, turnover and expense accounts. But once they had their bread and butter, they began to suffer the diseases of affluence.

A man was going to open the window but, when he fell down, he needed no more fresh air—just a shroud. People would suddenly clasp their chest, there, on the left side; the pain spread up into their shoulder. It was as though their heart were being cut in two, a torment and unease, a feeling of nothingness that turned the lips blue. The blood vessels narrowed and died. Those who didn't die straight away took to their beds until death could attend to them. But the agony didn't have to attack just the heart; others suffered from cramps in the leg. They would be walking along on the street and then have to stop dead from the pain. To disguise their illness they would gawp down at the flower beds or pretend to be looking into the shop windows.

Doctors said that it came from the diet, from all that rich fatty food, from eating too well and eating for no reason. Many people had sugar in their blood. Their urine smelt sweet and their kidneys no longer functioned properly. Many women became infertile and had sores on their legs. Those who fell sick were parched with thirst, getting up at all hours of the night to quench the burning dryness in their mouths, their skin, dry of any sweat, crawled with itches. In some cases the torso bloated up while arms and legs stayed normal; they were accumulating abdominal fat. The diabetics were not allowed bread, millet or groats. If they weren't careful, they went blind in old age, that is if they hadn't already fallen into a deep and terminal coma.

But it wasn't just a matter of diet, not just a question of the body failing to adapt to the good times and prosperity. The stresses and strains of career and success could also be killers. Many people were promoted to extra duties that caused physical duress; every excitement brought them a little closer to death, they suffered from high blood pressure and poor circulation. Career and family, salary and meetings had especially harmful effects on those conscientious souls who made the extra effort to rise to their responsibilities. Gastric fluid can digest all kinds of meat, and one day it digested the stomach lining itself. At first, sufferers would only notice heartburn and occasional vomiting, but then, one day, the stomach began to bleed and their vomit contained black–brown lumps. For which reason everyone took care to go about their business more calmly and with no great upsets, as long as this didn't lead to losses.

But the sicknesses that killed them were not always painful. Many carried a tumour around inside them, at work, at mealtimes, as they travelled or as they made love, the tumour was always there. Only when it grew into sensitive tissue would the tumour's host notice that he was sick. The tumour grew according to its own laws, malignant and out of control, it grew through anything that stood in its way, spread into every tissue and every bone, struck root in the liver and the oesophagus, in the skin and the lungs. When the autopsies were done, the pathologists could see how the tumour had run riot, metastasizing everywhere. This was how the draughtsman had started his sudden decline, with a feeling of repletion and a distaste for meat, even though he had always been a great meat-eater; he had always been the life and soul of the party, with his sea-blue eyes, and now he became pale, lost weight, complained of feeling tired as soon as he woke up in the morning, and died before his wife and children had even thought of death, in the midst of life and at the height of his career.

Yes, causes of death had changed in Mesopotamia but things had also changed for Noah; a stifling heatwave lay over all Mesopotamia as he moved into the Ark.

As the oldest, Shem had wrangled for himself and his family the right to choose their rooms first. He settled on a suite in the innermost recesses of the Ark. His wife insisted on bringing their furniture along; she was sentimentally fond of her trousseau, even though many pieces had been replaced over the years. Shem shoved beds and chairs about in the dark at her command or whim which changed from moment to moment; she wanted the table further to the right and the wardrobe further along from the door. Once the furniture was finally in place or, rather, back in the place where it had already been a while ago, Shem collapsed into a chair but then immediately sprang up again; curled up on the seat was a hedgehog. Enraged, he was about to throw the door back on its hinges when his wife screamed; a bird had built its nest above the door. Shem could see nothing in the dark but a lark flew out and fluttered around. Shem fumbled his way down the corridor and walked into some animal that hissed at him; he was almost hit in the face with a wing but the bat swerved to avoid him and then hung upside down on a beam. 'And we're trying to save this circus!' Shem yelled but no one could hear him for the squealing of pigs; he drew a deep breath and it smelt of goat. He went above, and once he was on deck he sketched in the empty air the space that he thought his family would need, but a whitish-yellow drop splattered on his finger as he pointed; he had chosen a spot next to the dovecote.

While he was looking for wood and cursing the tidiness with which the workers had cleared away all the offcuts and lumber, his two children came to him in tears and held out their little hands. 'We've been bitten,' they wailed. When their father asked what had bitten them, they shrugged; all they knew was that it was some horrid animal. When their father asked where, they pointed abaft. Then their father gave them each a clip around the ear, since he had expressly forbidden them to go near the beasts of prey. The children ran screaming to their grand-mother who hugged them and comforted them twice over, once for the bite and then once for the boxed ears. She gave them each an apple, blew onto their bites and promised that once they stopped crying they could have a ride on the elephants.

Noah's wife was right in the middle of making a garden. She had claimed a little patch on the tween decks and told no one what she needed it for. Nor had she asked any of the men for a favour. She brought soil onto the Ark by the basketful. 'They can laugh all they like,' she told herself to stiffen her resolve, 'they'll be glad of a few greens every now and then alongside all the dried food and pickles.' She shook out the soil into the beds she had pre-pared, crumbled the clods between the palms of her hands and raked it all over with her fingers spread. She was irked to find a stone in her soil and threw it up and away; it soared above the deck and then plummeted down into the depths over the Ark's side. 'Merciful God, there might be someone down there,' Noah's wife said in horror, clung to the rails and peered over; only then did the stone hit down below and she heard cursing. She realized just how high up her garden was. She paced out the size of the beds, thought of her earlier garden and then decided she would plant some flowers as well.

Then Japheth ran up to her. 'Where's the sheep?' He had leapt up the last few steps in one jump. 'You're not letting sheep run about up here,' said Noah's wife indignantly. 'A sheep got away from me,' Japheth admitted, and let his arm drop so that the cleaver almost slipped from his finger. Then Noah's wife noticed rabbits nibbling at her seedlings and clapped her hands, shooing them away. But when she tried to get back to her gardening, a monkey had taken the basket of seedlings and had it over his arm. It waited for her to approach, and then when she did, ran away dragging the basket behind itself so that seedlings jolted and jumped out at every bump. Noah's wife followed, shouting, threatening to beat the animal if she caught it and then keep it in chains for the duration. It let go of the basket scornfully, swung itself aloft and did acrobatics on the spar. While Noah's wife was gathering up the seedlings she bumped into Japheth. 'He'd taken shelter with the six sheep that we're going to save,' he reported, 'but actually he's the evening feed.'

Japheth didn't want Shem's wife to have her own kitchen. He put her on the spot, telling her that it was much better if everyone cooked together, for otherwise they would never manage even one square meal a day for all. He had put a stop to the nonsense of leaving the animals locked up in the order they had first come aboard; all the carnivores were now together in one place. The women would have to look after the birds and poultry, he said. Shem's wife relented and scattered the birdseed and chicken feed but she was offended by his tone and no longer gave her brother-in-law, Japheth, the time of day. 'All the same to me,' said Japheth, 'I just want some peace and quiet for my wife, she's pregnant.' He took no notice of his sister-in-law's behaviour and found new bones to pick with her; she should take better care of her children who had taken the name tags from all the stalls and cages, losing them and mixing them up. Noah's mother came to her grandchildren's defence, saying that they were only children after all, though she had to admit that it would be no good if all the animals had the wrong names in the end.

Ham was the only one who didn't care about his quarters; most of the time he slept outside the Ark. When push came to shove, he decided no one would get any rest anyway. Since he didn't lift a finger to help with either the feeding or the quarters, he had time on his hands. He knew a lot about the animals; he would prowl through the Ark, watching them sleeping and feeding, run experiments to see how they reacted to being called or being teased. 'Here's an odd animal,' he said in surprise on one of these tours and counted the legs again. 'Seventeen, indeed. What's it doing with seventeen legs!' He bent down to read the name tag and saw 'Strutphut'. All six of the strutphuts were scurrying about the cage, with no apparent rhyme nor reason, but five of them always following the sixth. Their tails stood straight up in the air and sometimes they waved their tails at one another, huddled together and then scattered and ran onwards. Ham took a stick and poked about between the bars. The strutphuts cowered at the back of the cage in a neat little row. They drew in their legs, all but one, on which they supported their heads, but then they drew their heads in too, leaving only a little dome showing at the top of the skull, a bump or a bulge. Ham shoved the stick further in and poked the animals; they opened a hole on each flank and sprayed out a thin jet of liquid. Ham pushed the stick against the head of the first animal which burst with a loud 'Phut!' and then shrivelled away, whereupon Ham burst the other five as well, saying, 'In future, no more strutphuts.'

He also had fun with the parrots. He let them out of the cage, tied a string to their legs so that they had enough freedom to fly but not so much that he couldn't haul them back in. He swaggered about with the six birds, not just in the Ark but through the streets, until his father noticed. Then Noah forbade his youngest son to take even a single animal from the Ark, except to take them to water. Ham taught the parrots to speak; once he reckoned that his lessons had stuck, he showed them off to his father. 'Say "deluge, deluge,"' he coaxed them, and all six of them moved their heads from left to right and then from right to left. Then Ham plucked a blue feather from one and held it in front of its beak, all the while repeating the word 'deluge'. The parrot fluttered up into the air, lost another feather, then settled back on Ham's shoulder and screeched, 'Dare huge . . . dare huge . . .' 'Don't pluck my parrots,' Noah snarled at his son. 'They'll learn,' said Ham soothingly, 'they'll say it right before I've plucked them naked. Listen! they can croak "Noah" on their own.' At the word 'Noah' all six parrots raised their heads, stabbed the air with their beaks and screeched the two syllables over and over, ceaselessly, 'No-ah, No-ah!'

Noah no longer dared go down into the belly of the Ark because of the smell, but he sawed and drilled airholes, not with the same care and attention that he had demanded from his workers, not caring whether the holes were neatly rounded or not, if only the heavy, stinking air could escape and no water could get in. When an airhole was ready, Noah would peer through; he could see all the new buildings crowded up against the Ark in rank and file, and in front of them a shock troop of scaffolding marking where the next blocks were to go up, which however had been standing there for a while; the turf had been stripped away and trenches dug for the foundations, with brick and timber lying piled up nearby. He didn't just look through the holes, he also pressed his mouth against them; his head throbbed and ached when he spent hours down there in the pens. Once he had put in airholes everywhere, he lifted doors off their hinges so that the wind could get into the belly of the Ark, but no wind blew. It still wasn't bearable but perhaps it was a little less unbearable, Noah decided, but when he tried to go above he could hardly lift his foot out of the muck, it was sunk in to the ankle. 'Well, you can't save their lives and then resent their bowel functions,' he had said defensively, of all the manure. But while he had been busy sawing airholes, the tide of dung had risen. At first he had reckoned that he wouldn't be able to get hold of enough fodder but many people had promised to let him have their scraps and leftovers for free, as long as he would collect it from their houses. Now, it turned out that he could feed the animals but not get rid of their droppings. He carried it upstairs with a pitchfork but by the time he came above, only half the forkful was left; he had scattered and splattered the rest of it on the way, in the corridors and on the stairs, and it took him half a day to empty even one pen. He could Ark-train the dogs and the cats by rubbing their noses in their mess until they learnt to leave the Ark to empty their bowels. But that was only a few animals, relatively speaking. He opened up one of the side doors again and let the animals out, as many as they could corral back into the Ark again in a hurry. He decided to saw some holes for the dung so that they only needed to shovel the muck out at the side. For if manure was left lying, the liquid could seep down into the timbers and the decks would rot. So he sawed another set of holes and unloaded the dung from there, and once he had cleaned out a row of pens he went above and leant on the railing. Then he saw that only part of the manure had fallen and the rest of the muck was dribbling slowly down the sides of the Ark, drying in the heat and then catching the rest as it fell. The Ark was scabbing over with a crust of stinking dung.

Noah's opponents got together, deciding that they wouldn't put up with it any longer. The complaints weren't just from the neighbours either. It had become impossible long before to sell land by the Ark site for development; quite the opposite, the houses that had been built there were now standing empty. Depending which quarter the wind stood in, the ammoniac stench could be smelt deep inland in Mesopotamia and on both rivers. There was no doubt as to where the stink came from; it was an unfamiliar stench, repellent and odd, and everyone congratulated themselves on having handkerchiefs at the ready. It smelt of animals that no one knew, although it was also quite obvious what was making the smell, the air was laden with excrement. People were almost happy to catch a whiff of something familiar in the foul air, and to declare, 'That's goats.' The air was pestilent and unclean and the smell got

worse every day. Wherever you went in Mesopotamia the air was so thick that no one batted an
eyelid when the men started to apply scent as well.
Anyone with a nose had only one thing to say.
'It reeks.'

The first to come out and oppose Noah were
the army. Fewer and fewer young men were volun-
teering for military service. The fathers spoke to the
young people at length, golden reminiscences of their
own time in the barracks and on the field of duty,
the trials they had undergone and the discipline they
had learnt. The young ones though, were not persuaded that it would strengthen their body or do
good to their souls to march with full kit for miles at
night, to stand ramrod straight under the burning sun
and to struggle with thirst as they stood by a foun-
tain; they reckoned the fracas of their daily life was
quite enough to be going on with. They grinned as
they listened to their fathers recall their days of glory,
how they had sprung out of bed at the first shrill of
the whistle, hurling themselves face down into a
gravel pit a quarter of an hour later. The young people cared not a jot for that special feeling that you
get when you put on a uniform, preferring to spend
the year-and-a-half that military service demanded
earning money instead. When told in imploring

tones that the fatherland needed sons, they conceded that they were willing to make said sons.

But the barracks had been expanded; parade squares and training grounds stood half-empty; assault courses had been fitted out with the most expensive tricks and cunning traps; an artificial swamp had been laid out to practice wading through. New uniforms were designed to be more attractive, recruits were promised a weekly bath and their wage was raised. In the end, the armed forces had no choice but to fix a quota for service and conscription by lottery. Most of the young men whose number came up, though, arrived at their draft assessment with a sworn statement or medical certificate; they were short-sighted or had dependents; they were suffering from post-traumatic stress disorder, or had an attention deficit and couldn't obey or give orders; they suffered from chronically sweaty feet; they were latent homosexuals. Many of them married, since married men were exempt from the draft; once the call-up was then widened to include husbands, many decided that it was time to become fathers. Those who had sharp eyes and healthy hearts though, those who didn't have a medical discharge or other exemption, almost exclusively volunteered for the river fleet which had rafts.

It was the commander of land forces who spoke out first, a soldier who had grown grey in the service, a bachelor well known for his curt criticism and grudging praise, who demanded that his men give their all, who crept through the mud with them on training but who also let them catch their breath when they had to. He spoke to a small audience of volunteers and addressed them as 'troops'. Despite his rank, he said, despite all his stripes and pips, he remained a soldier as he always had been. He despised patriotic phrase-making, yet for him the flag was more than just a piece of cloth, he wasn't ashamed of his tears, he was man enough to shed them. He had never fretted about having to hand over his command to someone else one day, as a soldier he lived to serve and to obey, but now it was becoming a grave concern that there may not even be anyone left to whom he could entrust his duties, his responsibility to keep order—indeed, if not for this small corps of men before him now, it would be more than a concern, it would be sheer desperation. They could rule out the idea that soldiers would be given porters and nail files. He had never demanded the impossible, he said; the two rivers of Mesopotamia flowed in meandering curves and he had never ordered them to flow zigzag. But this was a beautiful country. In peacetime, even the most watchful eye can droop and it was possible to lose a peace by sleeping too peacefully. During the last flood, even those who mocked the men in uniform had been happy that the soldiers were there, unafraid of infection, not caring about hours and overtime, simply there, there for Mesopotamia. He knew that young people today were no different from earlier and he didn't want to accuse them of anything. If there were accusations to be made, then against himself, against his generation. For it was their fault that these young people had been led astray. How else could a man be tolerated who didn't have the guts to say it in public but whose every act showed that he thought it—'Why defend Mesopotamia when soon enough there won't even be a Mesopotamia?'

Noah, confronted in the street and pressed for an answer, apologized for his poor memory, saying that he could no longer quite remember why he had been declared unfit for service but that his family had always lived in Mesopotamia and he was himself a Mesopotamian. Then Noah drew himself up and argued that since he never insisted that anyone else be patriotic, why were they all so keen that he should serve some fatherland? Strictly speaking, he hadn't lived there for a long time.

The Church took up the military's denunciations and took them further. 'That this land should choose to live in peace with itself,' the priest said in his opening words to the faithful, and he asked the old women and children to pass on his words to their sons, their husbands and fathers. 'A peace unbroken by prattle or music or the godless dancing of today. Noah is just the expression of a blasphemy and all are guilty who do not oppose it. This country has never been without spot or blemish but always we have tried to be virtuous. But where is virtue today? In the belly, not on its knees. Love in this country dwells between the thighs, not in the heart. This country thinks with its bowels, not with its head. The Flood was a warning but who has heeded it? No one! We gave way to panic, deciding that Noah may be half right after all, even if he was a quarter wrong. But, one day, Heaven will send no more warnings and the punishment itself shall fall, and each must face the question: What did I do about Noah?'

The architect whom Noah had first consulted about the Ark always stressed that he had had his reasons at the time for turning down the commission; he could remember very well how the others had laughed at him then, but he could never have

squared it with his conscience to take part in an enterprise where Noah had now become the victim. Nor
did the architect keep quiet about the psychologist,
saying how surprised he was that surely the good
doctor must have seen where things were headed.
The psychologist, though, flatly rejected any such
slurs on his good character and his professional abil-
ity; he had witnesses, he said, who had seen him plead
unsuccessfully with Noah on the street, to continue
treatment. If Noah had carried on with consul-
tation then building the Ark could have been the
therapy that it was so suited for; Noah was one of
those patients who could heal themselves by building
their own clinic, but now the Ark had turned out to
be a madhouse where Noah had shut himself away
out of sheer stubbornness.

The draughtsman's widow felt victimized by this
sort of talk and hid her face behind a chic, mourning
veil that she wore even after the prescribed period
was over; she did not want to see the memory of
her husband, father of her children, sullied. Obedi-
ently, no one said anything bad about the draughtsman, sticking to the principle that they should not
speak ill of the dead. The timber merchant was quick
to speak up for the draughtsman, a man he had
come to know as a dependable partner even at the

most testing times in the crisis. The timber merchant's word counted all the more since he had himself voiced his doubts right from the beginning, but he lived, he said, by the tradesman's creed and the popular wisdom that said a contract is a contract. Admittedly, he never foresaw that the Ark would one day become a stinking disaster, but to err is human, which was as true for himself as it was for everyone else, and he didn't blame them either. On one thing he stood firm though, that as soon as it became clear how Noah was leading them all by the nose, he had taken a stand then and there. If his daughter was living on the Ark today, then this was against his will, his daughter, he complained, had been misled if not abducted, and since that moment he had never set foot on the site, never mind on the Ark itself.

The lawyer concurred. He had long since retired from professional life and was enjoying the twilight of his days, gardening and reading, and since his last stroke had lived a very sheltered life; but this turn of events seemed to him to demand a response. His eyes were bright and alert as he spoke, though his voice trembled. 'I always argued, and even now that I am an old man I do not cease to argue, that everyone should be granted the same rights and freedoms.

But I argue equally strongly against the abuse of these rights. At the time, I spoke out in public, having nothing to hide, and those who hear me today will surely remember how I defended Noah as long as he did nothing to the detriment of others. When the animals arrived, I advised Noah to take certain safety precautions, and without me many of these precautions would simply never have been taken and the disaster would have been even greater. At the time, I took Noah to task, even at the risk of losing my best client. When Shem went to court in Yegerom, I got in touch with the appropriate authorities and let them know that I would not object to any proceedings that may be undertaken against Noah. That was my real mission. Could I have said so openly at the time though, and should I have said so? Given the widespread hysteria about Noah? I would have been driven out of town, and what then? Who would have taken over from me and talked behind the scenes? Now, of course, everyone can claim that they saw what was coming, now that you don't need to use your head in the matter but just have to follow your nose. Who would have kept their eyes open in my place? I expect no thanks but nor will I permit myself to be slandered, certainly not by those who until very recently were enjoying a carefree and self-indulgent lifestyle.'

One man was worried by all this talk, whose name had not even been mentioned at first, Erim. He hardly dared show himself in company, and likewise forbade his wife to meet the other wives. He had heard that the naturalist had not been made director of the National Institute, ostensibly because being independently wealthy he had no need of a post which would benefit others more, but everyone knew that he had in fact been denied this prestigious academic appointment because he had supplied Noah with the digest of Creation, at no charge, as he boasted. And Erim considered: What will happen to me then, when such a prominent man can be punished, a man with money too? One day, Erim's name was indeed mentioned. In everyone's eyes, in everyone's words, he was the guilty party, the pure profiteer who could argue no mitigating circumstances, a coward and toady who had not for nothing been released early from the institution, a man with no character; just at that very moment when Erim had boasted that he was ready to work, what had really been needed was steadfast refusal, and Erim could have refused more easily than anyone since he had nothing to lose.

Along with all these arguments the animal lovers also mounted a concerted campaign. You didn't need to go near the Ark to hear the animals roaring and howling, bleating and stamping. Everyone could imagine how the animals were being held; without sunlight, herded together, poorly fed, with no opportunity to exercise, dirty, mangy and with lice in their fur. One lady who kept dogs had crept into the Ark, had almost not found her way out again, and suffered headaches for days from all the noxious fumes; her speech was incoherent at first, but once words came back to her, she reported the horrors she had seen: animals moaning with no one coming to check up on them, troughs without water; proud eagles with lamed wings and gazelles lying apathetically behind bars; the king of beasts reduced to a broken-down predator; foxes that broke out and snatched the neighbours' geese; dogs attacking one another and snakes slithering about freely; mares foaling with no one there to help; skinny underfed sheep standing bleating as they waited for the slaughter. Mesopotamia had never seen such acts of animal cruelty.

The disquiet and protests spread as the heat grew ever more unbearable. The meteorological office had said that there was no change in sight for a long while yet. Schools were closed for the duration; people collapsed on the street as though struck by lightning, but they died of sunstroke. The harvests threatened to fail and the talk was not of a deluge but of drought. The insurance companies declared that they were ready to cover all costs if the state would agree to survey and examine all the wells and cisterns, to secure the water supply. There was a hosepipe ban in the gardens and a ban on baths in the houses, with water rationed for meals as well; only children and old people got an extra ration. Animals were also allowed water each day. Once people learnt how much water Noah was using, the heads of families were up in arms. Certainly, Noah could claim that he was taking much less than his due, but this changed nothing about the fact that in a period of shortage his Ark was using more water than a mid-sized village. Everyone was agreed, even before they debated the question, that the Ark had to go. It was more than a nuisance, it was a national embarrassment, a dungheap, a shame and a crime, a fart in the citizen's face and an insult to every right-thinking person—opinions were voiced slightly differently according to different classes and levels of education but were always the same. Like-minded people understood that they would not be content while the Ark still stood. It could be seen from all over. It was the biggest building in Mesopotamia. It was a blot on the landscape. The Ark was there as people woke up and there when they went to bed. If you couldn't see it, you could certainly hear it or smell it. The Ark was there at every dance and at every prayer, at every meal and declaration of love, at work and after hours.

'If we close the Ark,' the Mesopotamians pondered, 'then all this talk of a deluge will stop as well.'

'Close the Ark,' said the timber merchant to himself as he tossed and turned in bed at night. These days it wasn't like when he was young, when he had lain awake with columns of figures and bottom lines whirling through his head; as he grew older, he grew tired more easily but couldn't get to sleep. 'Yes,' he pondered, smoothing out his pillow, 'couldn't we make something useful of the Ark, something all Mesopotamia can enjoy? Haven't they had school classes visiting the Ark for lessons? But since the animals were locked away, you can't go visiting the kangaroo and the gnu.' He worked out in his head how much the Ark would be worth if it could be bought back. 'It could be an attraction. They used to come from the back of beyond to see the Ark. A word in Noah's ear, and who knows? It would be my chance to patch things up with Esther as well. There's something to be said for the Ark—

Noah's Ark, all the wonders of Nature in one place, entrance fee applies.'

The Ark became a scandal, no two ways about it. People succumbed to a fever with red pimples breaking out all over their skin; the sufferers scratched till they bled, and the fever abated then came back again, and no herbal tea or cold compress could help. The doctors were baffled and discussed the matter, then it was found that all these people had been drinking water from the same well. The water board sent down a man who came back up with six animal corpses which were immediately sent to the National Institute. The investigation lasted so long that people began to call it a cover-up, and then it was announced that these were strutphuts. Exotic, strange and very rare animals from the Ark; Noah had poisoned the well.

'I've had enough of all the complaints,' Noah told his family. He had asked them all to come and now they were astonished not at his words but at how he looked. He hadn't just shaved his scalp bare but his eyebrows too, and when Shem asked him, 'Why?' Noah answered, 'The pubic hair's gone too.' Noah's wife put her hands over her grandchildren's ears but there were four ears and she only had two hands. Noah showed them the knife that he had whetted and told Ham to sit down in front of him. Noah's wife bustled the grandchildren away but they fought back, wanting to watch. Noah promised to shave their heads too. Shem's wife and Japheth's wife fell into one another's arms, hugging tighter than they ever had since they'd come onto the Ark, gazing at one another's hairdos. Shem demanded an explanation and then began to scratch; his hand leapt hither and yon through his hair. 'Wait, I'll help,' Noah's wife told him. Shem lowered his head, his mother ran her fingers through his mane and hunted about with her thumbnails, stopped for a moment, pinched them closed and wiped away the wingless little beast on her apron. 'That's an itch that I don't have to scratch any longer,' declared Noah. 'But we wash, we do!' protested the women. 'The lice don't go away just because you wash. Why are you so fond of them?' Noah shot back, holding the knife to Japheth's arm, 'We've enough fleas and bugs to be going on with.'

Everyone shaved themselves bald or let the others shave them. Noah's wife collected the women's hair as a memento, and also to stuff cushions. They were still scratching themselves for a while after, not because of flea bites but because they had nicked and scraped the skin. The first time Ham showed up in public as a skinhead, several people believed that he was setting a new trend; everyone who copied his look ended up most embarrassed once they heard that Ham was going about all shaven and shorn because of the lice.

Once, when Noah was sitting at the meal table, he broke out into uncontrollable laughter. The women had taken off their headscarves and tossed their head back a little, just like earlier when they would sweep the hair away from their neck and forehead; this time, though, there was no hair to flick away. The hairline was quite clearly visible across the back of the head, marking off a patch of paler skin. Noah had never seen all the bare scalps together in one place before; they looked new, for until now the hair had always disguised the shape of everyone's head. Noah watched all heads dip down towards the plates and dishes, looking more like skulls than living heads. He left the Ark. As he stepped off the gangway at the bottom, he found a grandson. The boy had dug a hole and filled it with water, then set a bit of tree bark floating, laden with stones; he puffed out his cheeks and blew, and then swore when the water seeped away from his sea.

Noah hid, choosing a spot where he had off-loaded all the iron rations that had gone bad, intending to bury them later. This was where he had chucked out the maggot-ridden millet, and also where he had rolled the barrels full of spoilt grape juice. He loved grapes and half of them he had dried, calling the dried grapes 'raisins'—sweet, even if the pips were over large and tended to stick between the teeth. The other half, though, he had pressed, getting a sticky, sweet juice. But once he came to inspect the rations, he found that the juice had turned, becoming sour and foul-tasting, and he had rolled out those barrels to the rest of the spoilt supplies where now he was seeking a little peace and quiet.

When he leant up against the barrel, the scratch-marks on his back stung; the stuff was sticky, and he stood straight again, wiping the sweat away from his forehead. He unwound the bandage from his hand and squeezed at the weeping wound there, felt the pain as the pus broke forth from the skin; he pressed down on the wound until blood and water flowed out after it. Then he held the wound out in the sun, slumped down and fell asleep.

When he opened his eyes, he was looking at a pair of shoes. Puzzled, he shuffled about on the ground and peered behind the barrels. A young man lay there, Mesopotamian but not a local, asleep. One hand had opened up as he slept and Noah saw two flints lying in the palm, noticed a fresh pile of wood-shavings and rags behind him. Two dogs launched themselves towards the stranger who awoke with a start. Noah called off the dogs who had their forepaws up on the intruder and were barking. Only when Noah raised his hand did they come to heel but they kept sniffing and straining at the stranger, not taking their eyes off him. The stranger raised himself up on one elbow and said in greeting, 'The king of the con men, Noah.' Noah stayed where he was. 'Oh yes, the Ark beats forging signatures,' said the stranger, nodding in admiration, and pointed to the Ark, 'you can get a life sentence for that.'

Noah asked him where he had come from, pushing away the dogs who were licking at his bandage. 'Been bitten?' asked the stranger, laughing, and carried on talking. 'From Yegerom, if you can imagine that. That's where my family lived anyway. And if I hadn't been serving out hard labour in the quarries, I would have drowned along with my nearest and dearest. You see, you can't be too careful. So you're Noah. Do you know how much the convicts admire you? Let everyone drown, and then off and away on an Ark. What's an armed robber or a mugger compared to you? Not to mention me with my embezzlement.' He clenched a fist around his flints. 'But I think you're scum—the Flood could have been such a great idea.'

'I don't have an animal like you on board,' said Noah cheerily. Then the stranger pointed a finger at Noah, as though pointing him out for an audience. 'You're not rescuing the animals, the animals are rescuing you. You're smuggling yourself on board the Ark among all your beasts. It could be anyone else mucking out and minding the pens during the Flood. Be honest about it, why not just go into the great crate on your own? Isn't your own family a good enough excuse? But you know in your bones that you're not worth saving on your own—everything standing there stinking and bellowing behind us is just an excuse. You believe you deserve damnation, you just don't want that sentence carried out.' The stranger snapped his fingers so that the dogs began growling. Noah nodded 'yes' with his head and shrugged 'no' with his shoulders, patted the dog that lay next to him and scratched the fur of the other. 'I never believed in the Flood, it just seems right to me. I don't do what I do out of conviction, just from observation and deduction.'

'You don't understand what the Ark is,' said Ham, joining the conversation. Noah and the stranger both looked up in surprise. Ham came closer, swinging his arms. 'Congratulations,' he said to the stranger with a bow. 'Father never talks to us like this. We're just rescued and that's that. Yes,' turning to Noah, 'down here by the barrels, that's where we find you. Good that you're talking about it. I don't want to interrupt but this young man hasn't quite understood what the Ark is about.' Noah continued to stroke the dog. Ham lifted his arm and pointed at the Ark. 'This is the great copulation of every living thing that creeps and flies, everything that breathes and feeds. I don't know whether my father even suspects what he has created. He thinks that afterwards everything will carry on as before—with the same old inbreeding. Man will beget man and the camel the camel. Why build the Ark, then? It only makes sense if all the seeds inside it are mixed together. So far man has only ever thought in terms of man but why not invent something else? Give him a paw from the lion so that when he strikes, he slays, and give him the suppleness of the serpent so that he can twist and turn like never before and so that nothing can get to him. He should have the elephant's hide and the scorpion's sting so that he needn't backbite but can strike and kill stone dead. That's the plan for afterwards. Our children's children shall be nothing but monsters, instantly recognizable, chimaera.'

'No one would build an Ark on Ham's account but we're taking him along,' explained Noah, making his youngest son burst out laughing. 'You come too,' Noah offered the stranger. The stranger's face froze and then the corners of his mouth drooped. 'Bribery!' And then the stranger joined in Ham's laughter, spluttering and coughing, 'Excuse me, I should pick my words more carefully. My codefendant embezzled the same amount as I did but he was acquitted, he had a bigger vocabulary. Come along, come with you, just because I've seen through you. No, Noah. I'll drown with a clear conscience. I'll wave to you.' He looked at Noah, and Noah drew back his foot to hide the swollen ankle; straw and dung clung to his other foot. Noah shooed away the flies that were buzzing around his hand. The stranger stood up, straightened his robe and tossed the flints at Noah's feet. 'The worst thing about mankind is not that it perishes but that it survives.'

Noah watched the stranger walk away, then called after him. The stranger did not turn round however, not even when Ham set the dogs to fetch him. Noah got up, leaning on the barrel; his mouth was dry. He pried away some of the wood. He shuddered as he drank the spoilt juice, and spat but a curious taste lingered on his palate. He scooped up some more and washed his face; although the juice was warm and sticky, it felt cool. Noah lapped from the palm of his hand, his face wet from the nose down to the chin. He leant over the rim of the barrel, propped up on his elbows, put his face to the top of the juice and slurped and swallowed. He was surprised; the juice flowed down to his stomach but climbed to his head as well.

When he heard the animals roaring, he straightened up and lurched to one side. 'That's no rain, that's an earthquake.' He looked down at the ground. 'Why's it dancing?' He lifted one foot and nearly fell over. The juice ran down his chin and his throat and he felt sorry that he couldn't drink it in through his pores. The animals roared and mixed into the roaring was the bleating of sheep waiting for slaughter. 'If it could rain this stuff, the Flood would be great fun,' said Noah, goggling down into the barrel. 'You stop it, you beasts, or I'll drown you all.' He slapped his fist into the barrel and the juice splashed out at every blow. He grabbed at empty air as though catching something, and plunged his fist into the barrel. 'Got him.' And as the bubbles rose, Noah chuckled. 'He's blubbering.' He began to snatch one animal after another from thin air, his hands were bait, trap, net and pitfall; he lunged in all directions, snorting and barking, calling pet names and calling commands. He muttered a cheery litany, 'I drown the deer . . . I drown the goose . . . I drown the dog . . . I drown the snake . . . May the elephant be with you and with thy trunk . . . I drown the ox . . . I drown the giraffe . . . and just so the barrel doesn't run over, I'll take a swig after every animal drowns.' When he stretched out his arms to drown whole stalls full of animals, he fell over; he grabbed for a handhold and clutched only the blue sky above.

When he woke, he saw the sun in a dark sky but the sun was a moon and the darkness was not a storm cloud but rather the night. Noah's stomach grumbled as though all the animals of the Ark were penned in there; he felt as though he were going to be sick but his stomach was empty. He fumbled about on the ground and realized that he hadn't fallen out of bed, rather he'd never even got into bed. The animal that had startled him was a barrel next to which he lay; and the pillow hadn't turned hard, it was a stone, and the cat's eyes watching him were two flints. His mouth burnt; he was amazed at this juice, that you could drink so much of it and feel thirsty afterwards. He felt a pressure in his bladder and relieved himself. The heap of tinder which the stranger had assembled the day before, collapsed under the stream. Chains rattled, a cock began to crow and others answered it, geese cackled, an animal stamped and the horses whinnied; the Ark was waking up. Noah sat down, put his head in his hands and sighed, 'If only I could mix a little sleep into the fodder for the Ark.' 'Fodder'—the word brought his eyes back into focus and gave him something to think about. Noah set off on his feed round.

He found no bucket in front of the first house, he even looked under the steps but to no avail. The moon grew pale and the sun turned yellow. No bucket stood at the door of the second house either; he looked down the street; all the spots where he usually picked up the feed-pails stood empty. When he heard crockery rattle, he knocked at the window where a highland Turk was preparing her family's breakfast, but before he could ask, she answered, 'No scraps todays, maybe tomorrow.' Noah considered whether he should walk his usual route or go straight to the restaurant, but there too he found nothing, just rings on the ground marking where the buckets had stood. The sun was casting its first hazy shadows. Noah decided to count off five houses and then ask what had happened. Hardly had he approached the door when it was opened from the inside, there stood a woman combing her hair. 'Haven't seen a woman's hair for a long time, have you?' she greeted Noah. 'Up and about so early?' 'Earlier than usual,' Noah replied. 'You wanted me to come and collect early.' 'Ah yes,' said the woman, as though remembering. 'Your feed round—and then you go and poison us.' The woman plaited her hair, holding her comb between clenched teeth. 'How stupid do you think we are?' she asked, the comb falling from her mouth. Noah stopped and picked up the comb, then the woman jumped back as she smelt Noah's breath. 'Taking our scraps to feed that Ark of yours.'

'You keep your rubbish,' scoffed Noah. Even though his ankles were giving him trouble as he walked, he strode along jauntily without looking left or right at the doors where the feed-pails usually stood; he didn't notice the heads jostling to see at the windows. 'Good,' he said to himself, thinking. 'As long as we still have supplies, we'll eat our way through those. After that I'll let the animals loose on one another. That way at least some of them will last out.' He snorted at the thought of the animals. 'I've been taking this society too seriously. What if it's not even worth the water it would take to drown it? And what if I've been overdoing it? What if Noah's gone too far? He whistled derisively at society and at himself. 'Society's pulled a fast one on you. There's no worm gnawing at the world, the world is the worm and we're inside.' 'Beg your pardon?' asked a passerby; Noah was taken aback and the other man smiled. 'I thought you said something.' 'Just humming a tune,' said Noah apologetically.

Erim let his valise fall from his hand when he saw Noah approaching the house. He called through the front door to his wife, 'Careful!' and spread his fingers in defence; two crooked teeth showed in his lower jaw. 'We're even.' Noah had stopped in front of the garden; he looked at the whitewashed walls and thought of the crust of dung on the Ark; he compared the trim little windows with the airholes he had sawn, admired the ornamental chimney breast and the working hearth. 'Just the right size, your house,' said Noah admiringly. 'It would have been a nice life in Mesopotamia,' Erim complained. He turned his face to the house and beamed for a moment, then pointed to the verandah roof, 'That's new. And fresh gravel on the paths. But the others make life unpleasant.' 'Where are you going, Erim?' asked Noah. 'So that you can find me?' Erim shouted, enraged. 'I'm going so far away that I'll never see any of you again.' He pushed the bag between his legs and put one foot on top of it, as though he hadn't bought it but gone out and shot it. 'And that's why you bought this house?' asked Noah. 'Rented. Furnished. I would have had the use of it for free, if anybody cares,' Erim moaned. 'Far away,' Noah repeated and looked down the street. 'Further than that,' said Erim and Noah looked out over the rooftops into the dawn sky. 'I called that place the Ark.'

'You've got it easy,' Erim said bitterly, 'when the time comes, you just sit in your Ark and off you go.' 'Do you believe that it will rain?' asked Noah, stretching out his hands. 'We're all waiting for something to happen, and when it does we'll need an Ark,' Erim answered and glanced back to see whether his wife was listening at the door. Noah confessed with a merry twinkle that he had put the Flood behind him and no longer needed a place on the Ark. This remark upset Erim who got his own back at Noah by staring straight past him. Noah wanted to hear that the Mesopotamians were fighting for a place on his Ark, that they were coming to blows over the right to feed the animals. He had the wits to build an Ark, said Noah, but not to go aboard. By the time the eggs were collected from the chicken coops, he'd have a replacement. Erim shook Noah. 'Your eyes are shining.' Noah explained the gleam in his eyes by speaking of barrels and of rain, of himself and an unknown stranger. Then Erim demanded to know what the man would look like who would take over the Ark and whether he might look like himself. 'I'll give the Ark to the next man I meet.' 'And if the next man you meet is a former camel-drover?' Erim asked. 'Then the camel-drover will get away with it,' answered Noah. 'But I can't let you give me an Ark without giving something in return,' Erim told Noah and they both thought about it. Noah looked at the camel-drover's luggage and the camel-drover listed what he had packed there: necessities and food for a couple of days. Then Noah swapped his Ark for a valise.

'Good to see you, lovely morning,' said the timber merchant to one and all; he had risen early since he'd heard of an auction for a piece of land near the Ark site. Noah came down the street whistling and carrying a valise. 'Up so early and still cheerful,' the timber merchant said to Noah, and Noah returned the greeting, saying 'The wind's from another quarter now.' The timber merchant joined in his laughter, making sure to laugh just enough. Noah bumped his bag into the timber merchant's thigh as he set it down so that the merchant rubbed his leg as he listened carefully to Noah's words. 'Esther and Japheth. We'll be grandfathers again soon enough. Grandsons are everything that sons should have been. They never disappoint us, we die before that can happen.' 'You and your jokes,' said the timber merchant affably, then looked at Noah's swollen ankle and told him that he should take care and wanted to know whether he was taking a stroll, and if so, where. 'It's too hot for me to stay and wait for the Flood,' Noah answered. The timber merchant said that he reckoned Noah could have a nice life, if he knew what was what. The two of them sat down at the foot of someone's front steps; the timber merchant greeted all passers-by and Noah took his valise between his legs. 'Elegant,' said the timber merchant, approving of Noah's taste. 'If you just take the time for them, your friends will come back to you.' The timber merchant counted pebbles from one hand to the other, letting some of them slip through his fingers and lie where they fell. 'You changed the way we see the world,' he began. 'Without you, we would have no idea what's out there. The first time I heard tell of a cobra, I thought that it slithers along the ground like all the rest and then I saw it eating rabbits. It's just that I often wondered, and I've talked to other people about this as well, whether the Ark couldn't be a bit more spaciously laid out, a bit healthier for man and beast. The basic idea of bringing together all sorts of unknown animals in one place is sheer genius—like flypaper, we couldn't do without that these days. I'm thinking of a great big garden but not with flowers or trees, not with vegetables either, a garden with a selection of rare animals, which you can pay to visit.' Two children scampered down the steps hand in hand, one with her hair in a band and the other with his ringlets still smelling of the curling iron. The timber merchant stopped what he was saying and remarked on the innocence of childhood. The two children sang, 'Noah's got a moa, the poor bird can't fly but he keeps it dry.' Then the timber merchant scolded the two of them so that they almost fell off the stairs in surprise, asking whether they had no respect for their elders and betters. But Noah said soothingly, 'Those two don't know yet that the Ark belongs to Erim now.'

Once the timber merchant had said his goodbyes to Noah, he sent a messenger to the lawyer straight away; Erim was the new owner of the Ark. The lawyer sent a highland Turk to the priests to let them know the news; Noah had given up. The priests met for an impromptu conclave; Noah was ready to do penance. The timber merchant himself hurried to see the draughtsman's widow and tell her that a camel-drover, of all people, expected to be saved. The lawyer's clerk made his excuses and ran home to tell his wife that Noah had thrown in the towel. But his wife wasn't at home, she was already out telling a friend that Noah had washed his hands of the matter and, as the two of them were on the way to meet another of their circle, they met her at the door and she told them in turn that Noah had left the Ark high and dry. Turkish waiters told their landlords that Erim had paid a vast sum for the Ark; the landlords whispered to their guests that Noah was a rich man again, and the guests asked one another, 'Who gave Erim the loan?' The animal lovers celebrated the news as a triumph of philanthropy over egotism. The psychotherapist gave his diagnosis; Noah had suffered a shock. In the barracks, word was passed down the ranks: Noah's defeat marked just the beginning and there were other scores to settle with subversive elements. In the schools, the support staff came and knocked on the doors to ask the teachers for a moment, and, instead of resuming classes, the teachers gave a little lecture on how far a man can go. And everyone said that it was now safe to talk about the weather again.

Although no time or place was ever really agreed, later that morning everyone who had the time, which somehow included the nurses and the prison wardens, gathered in front of Erim's house. One man dragged another along with him and then the two of them persuaded a third to come too, only to find that that's where he was headed anyway. One group followed the next, deep in conversation, hectic. Road-mending gangs set down their tools. The hammering fell quiet on building sites. Whole factories demanded a morning's half-holiday. Shopkeepers padlocked their frontages and followed their customers. Instead of going home to cook lunch, the housewives turned up with their baskets and shopping bags. Children coming home from school followed the grown-ups. Since no one knew quite what the meeting was about, the tension mounted. Everyone listened eagerly to the old news and the new. Street traders mingled with the crowds to sell them drinks.

Then an author came to the front, with a scroll in his hand. The gossipmongers wanted to know what he was going to read out, and the highland Turks wondered who this skinny young man was, peering short-sightedly at the crowd. The author read out a list of names in his famous monotone drone. From time to time, he looked up at the priests standing off to one side with the police officers. The lawyer spoke up straight away, declaring himself ready to sign; he won loud applause by saying that, in this matter, writers and clergy, students and workers were all agreed. As the lawyer set pen to papyrus to write his name, the writer tore the scroll from his hand. The lawyer had been about to sign at the top but the writer explained that this was where the text of the protest, still being revised, would be inserted. Whereupon the lawyer signed his name below all the others.

A chant went up all of a sudden, 'Erim, Erim.' Youngsters flung stones at the camel-drover's house. When the first stone shattered a windowpane, they whooped. The priests sent the police in against the demonstrators, declaring that they had to keep things dignified, in fact the more dignified, the more effective the demonstration would be. At which, people in the crowd nodded to one another: That's it, we're at a demonstration. Someone had already stove in the door to Erim's house. While everyone waited for Erim to emerge from the house, he turned up behind the demonstrators. He shoved his way through an alley of tightly packed bodies, putting up no defence when hands plucked at his clothing from behind; he had a feed-bucket in each hand. 'What are you cooking?' shouted one young man, leaping at him and spitting into the pail, vanishing again behind a wall of onlookers. 'Swill,' someone shouted and someone else answered, 'Tasty.' Erim looked at his house; the garden path was blocked by women with children. Erim put the buckets down and wiped his brow; happy to have thought of the gesture, he repeated it. Then the lawyer stepped forwards and bowed without lowering his gaze. 'Very pleased to meet you—though I don't know whether I should congratulate you as the new owner of the Ark or offer my sympathies.'

'Go easy on him,' interrupted the Chief Constable. 'I want police protection,' Erim pleaded. 'He wants every pair of eyes arrested that dares look at him,' the lawyer said, scornfully. 'I'm here,' the Chief Constable told the camel-drover reassuringly, one hand at his belt where the ceremonial truncheon hung. Erim grabbed hold of the police officer who brushed his hands off his uniform. 'Whoever accepts the Ark, accepts all the consequences,' said the lawyer, turning to the Chief Constable; he beckoned to the crowd to listen. 'Erim is an upright citizen. He will compensate us for injuries suffered, even if only with his own house. At least with him we're not dealing with a well-poisoner—unless well-poisoning itself is infectious, like the poisoned water.'

The psychoanalyst snorted and said that it wasn't. The camel-drover nodded gratefully when he heard that even a camel-drover counts as human. 'If what's due to him is what was due to Noah, that means he also has to face the case we were bringing against Noah,' said the lawyer, cutting off all this debate. 'But,' he said, tapping his shoes with his walking stick, 'since Noah had the right to legal counsel, Erim is also entitled to a defence. My dear doctor, would you like to take over the defence? I am perfectly happy to act as prosecutor. And yourself, sir? Would you care to adjudicate?' The Chief Constable smiled. 'Ordinarily, people don't like to see us police acting as judges but if I can be of service then please go ahead!' The lawyer took a few steps towards the crowd. 'This trial does not need to be held in a courtroom, any more than the deluge can take place behind closed doors. This trial should be heard in public.' The crowd broke into applause and settled down for the show; some sat on the ground, the women produced fruit to eat, others stood with their arms folded. Since there was a pause, the spectators started clapping again. Then the Chief Constable opened the trial with the question,

'Counsel for the defence, what do you know of the accused?' At the same time, he told Erim to wipe that drop away from his nose; Erim got out his handkerchief and buried his face in it. 'He was released early from an institution . . .' remarked the psychiatrist, one hand on Erim's shoulder. 'Discharged? Institution? Please be more exact, my learned friend! Or what is my lord's opinion?' asked the lawyer. The Chief Constable stroked his belly and looked about. 'I'd like a chair.'

'Yes, the Ark belongs to Erim,' Noah confirmed. No one had noticed him join them. Everyone was amazed but the lawyer was most surprised of all. Noah was wearing sandals and had a white bandage wound about his right hand; his shaven skull gleamed. With one voice, the crowd let out a cry of astonishment. 'Noah has washed!' Erim lifted his head, having noticed nothing at first but the a strong smell of soap. 'And no trial will make any difference to Erim's going on the Ark instead of me. I gave him the Ark.' An 'Ah!' of amazement went through the crowd along with an envious 'Oh!' 'Do you have witnesses?' the Chief Constable asked Noah. The lawyer wanted to remind the judge that since Noah was speaking as a witness, he needed no further witnesses himself. But Noah was ready to answer the question; earlier that morning, he said, he had pawned a valise. He looked around at the spectators, looking for the pawnbroker and then for a shoe-maker—anyway, he said, he and Erim had made the exchange between themselves, 'under the clear blue sky'. The lawyer retracted his earlier point, saying pithily, 'If the clear blue sky is an acceptable witness than I shall subpoena the wind.'

Erim grabbed hold of Noah, whereupon the Chief Constable separated the two of them as they argued; he used his fists professionally and decisively but he took care to spare his uniform. Erim shouted that Noah was a 'swindler', a 'con man' and a 'char-latan'. Noah told Erim that this was no time to give up or lose his nerve, that he was giving him the Ark free and clear, for himself and his family, it really didn't matter who escaped as long as there was someone on board; as for himself, he only wanted one thing, he wanted to keep the barrels full of spoilt grape juice, and that was his only condition. Then Erim put the two feed-buckets in front of Noah, saying, 'Keep the whole Ark'. Putting up his guard, Erim took a few long steps backwards and ducked behind the Chief Constable. Noah took the two buckets and followed Erim; they ran around the Chief Constable, one carrying the buckets and the other running away from them. The Chief Constable called, 'Halt!' and Erim stopped dead so that Noah ran straight into him. Erim tore a bucket from his hand and emptied it over Noah's head. Scraps of bread stuck to Noah's face; he brushed leaves and fruit-peelings from his shoulders; a sour fluid dribbled down his robe and gnawed bones lay at his feet.

'You think I'd have fed your beasts? Given them water when we barely have anything to drink ourselves?' shouted Erim. 'I'd have slaughtered them.' The watching crowd roared. 'Very strange,' said the lawyer in loud amazement, 'A very strange trial. The witness turned defendant and the defendant became the plaintiff.' He approached the psychiatrist and took him by the arm. 'I admit that you have the right of it. We shouldn't be prosecuting Erim, we should be defending him. Now that Noah realizes what a ridiculous project his Ark was,' talking now to the priests, 'what an unsocial and inconsiderate enterprise,' talking to the workers, 'he wants someone else to take his place. Now Noah is ducking out since he finds he can't go on. And we were almost accomplices in this wicked ploy.'

The empty feed-pail stood on one side and the full one on the other. Noah stepped aside, turning to speak to those in front of him and those behind, to the left and to the right. 'If Erim gives back the Ark then I'll look for someone else to take over from him. I'm offering the Ark as is. I'm offering a good Ark—best-quality wood. The timber merchant will swear to it. Three storeys, with stables, hutches and cages, pens, a beehive and a dovecote. If you want to view the property first, please do so. Each one of you knows it already though. With the property comes enough land for the Ark to stand on. Going once, going twice . . .' Noah waited and looked at the crowd. 'The Ark can be had for free,' he began again, then a voice from the crowd heckled, 'Is the scratching included?' 'It's a once-in-a-lifetime chance,' called Noah, bellowing like a barrow boy, 'The Ark, with everything that lives on board, up for auction.' A stone landed on the ground behind him; Noah stepped closer to the crowd and they stepped back as they smelt his sour stench, and the children huddled closer to the grown-ups. 'No hidden catches, no jerry-building,' Noah implored them, 'not a panic sale, no down payment. Anyone can take the Ark. Do you only want it if your neighbour has one too? Bidding opens on the Ark. Going once . . . going twice . . . going to the devil!' Noah stood in the middle of a circle again; he climbed up on the empty bucket and held a hand above his eyes, 'No bids from the back of the crowd? Hay and soused meat included, jam and raisins. Don't trust the sky up there, it's only blue to deceive you. I'm offering the Ark for one last time.' He pointed at the crowd. 'Going once,' and he pointed upwards. 'Going twice,' and he pointed at himself. 'Going three times. You've all witnessed it. I hereby award Noah's Ark to Noah.'

'What do you look like!' said Noah's wife indignantly. 'And what on earth are you doing standing on the bucket?' She was carrying a basket of eggs over her arm. Feeling all eyes upon her, she asked in confusion whether she was interrupting something; she couldn't understand why all these people were standing about in the middle of the day. Since no one said a word but kept on staring, she was relieved to spot the timber merchant. She handed him the basket, told him how many eggs there were and said that she would let the money for the eggs mount up as before; when there was enough, he knew what she wanted, a cradle, but not the usual design, one with little hearts all around it, so that she could tie the children to it once they were standing and walking. Esther would be so happy to see it, she told him, and it was a shame that he hadn't made it to the wedding. Since the timber merchant didn't say a word, and nor did anyone else, she described the wedding festivities and then turned to her husband. 'What do you look like, Noah. And away all night. What a day it's been. One of the cows has calved, Ham's parrots have flown off and the frogs have climbed all the way up to the dovecote. Shem and Japheth don't have any feed-pails and here's one tipped out all over the ground. Come along, Noah. We have to feed the animals.'

As Noah climbed down and stretched out his hand, one of the priests whispered loudly so that every syllable could be heard, 'If Noah were not well known to want the Flood, you might think he were one of the righteous of the earth.' 'What's to become of him?' asked the psychiatrist. 'First we'll liquidate the Ark,' suggested the lawyer. 'Liquidate,' repeated the Chief Constable shocked, and the timber merchant gave his estimate of the value of the wood in the Ark. 'There'll be something left over for Noah as well,' said the lawyer, considering the figure. 'If not, we'll look after him ourselves.'

'The sons are old enough to look after themselves,' declared the Chief Constable. 'We'll find something for Noah to do. I know an opening. Not the cleanest, admittedly. But the highland Turks who refuse the job are exaggerating.' When everyone wanted to know what post he had in mind, the

Chief Constable gave them their answer. 'The post of public knacker.'

Noah took the full bucket and followed his wife. Voices cried out. Long-tailed creatures were creeping out of Erim's house and from all the houses nearby; the rats left the cellars and ran along the gutters, climbed over feet and shoes. They squealed when stamped on and scurried on; those that escaped the kicks and stones thrown at them came together into a column and flocked towards the Ark. Noah stumbled in the rush of rats. A wind sprang up; the noise and the stench hung heavy in the air. Noah walked on. One of those watching him leave said, 'Only the Flood can save him now.'